SOUTH & WEST YORKSHIRE

Edited by Ed Thompson

First published in Great Britain in 2016 by:

 Young**Writers**

Remus House
Coltsfoot Drive
Peterborough
PE2 9BF
Telephone: 01733 890066
Website: www.youngwriters.co.uk
All Rights Reserved
Book Design by Ashley Janson
© Copyright Contributors 2016
SB ISBN 978-1-78624-177-1

Printed and bound in the UK by BookPrintingUK
Website: www.bookprintinguk.com

FOREWORD

Enter, Reader, if you dare...

For as long as there have been stories there have been ghost stories. Writers have been trying scare their readers for centuries using just the power of their imagination. For Young Writers' latest competition Spine-Chillers we asked students to come up with their own spooky tales, but with the tricky twist of using just 100 words!

They rose to the challenge magnificently and this resulting collection of haunting tales will certainly give you the creeps! From friendly ghosts and Halloween adventures to the gruesome and macabre, the young writers in this anthology showcase their creative writing talents.

Here at Young Writers our aim is to encourage creativity and to inspire a love of the written word, so it's great to get such an amazing response, with some absolutely fantastic stories. We will now choose the top 5 authors across the competition, who will each win a Kindle Fire.

I'd like to congratulate all the young authors in *Spine-Chillers – South & West Yorkshire* – I hope this inspires them to continue with their creative writing. And who knows, maybe we'll be seeing their names alongside Stephen King on the best seller lists in the future...

Jenni Bannister

Editorial Manager

CONTENTS

Notre Dame High School, Sheffield

Sheffield Springs Academy, Sheffield

Tapton School, Sheffield

The McAuley Catholic High School, Doncaster

Yewlands Academy, Sheffield

THE MINI SAGAS

Below

At night, when the ship fell silent and nought was heard but the creaking of the timbers, a sound came from below. *Knock!* From the ship's bell it beckoned. *Knock!* Down, down far below. *Knock!* In the dark, a man crept in search. *Knock!* In search of the disquieting din. *Knock!* Behind a panel in her belly, a sound echoed from within, *Knock!* He broke the panel. *Knock!* From a hook, a hammer swung. *Knock!* At last, he caught the hammer. Silence. Lightwards, the man fled. *Tap... tap... tap...* everywhere and nowhere. *Knock!*

Victoria Smith (15)

Mirror Alive

Hannah's fingers traced against the smooth engraved wood around the mirror. Her mum had warned her never to touch it. But she was dead now, though nobody had ever found her body. As her palm touched the mirror's surface, a face appeared. A face with blood down one side, the other side hidden behind tangled hair. 'Hannah,' an unearthly voice called, 'I see it is your turn to meet your end.' A hand with claw-like nails suddenly grasped Hannah's neck tighter and tighter until blood dripped. Hannah screamed, but no one heard, for she was already pulled into the mirror.

Anshrah Adeel

The Creepy Castle

As I enter the porch of the weird-looking, deserted castle, the decayed door creaks open. My heart pounding with anxiety, I turn to walk away when a strong gush of wind pushes me into the castle. The door slams shut. 'Let me out,' I shout. No response! 'Be brave, be brave,' I reassure myself. I drag my trembling feet up the metal spiral staircase. Light rays beneath the closed door pull me closer to the room. Familiar voices are echoing. Turning the cold, rusty door handle I push my way in. What I see will never be repeated...

Salis Riaz (12)

The Ghost Boy

There is a grave of a man. The man was the husband to the woman in black. The woman in black placed blood-red roses on the grave. The woman in black stood as a huge cloud of fog crept in towards the grave. As she turned she heard a... *crack!* It was the grave of the husband. Stood behind was a dead boy screaming, 'You shall die!' Then the grave shattered into millions of pieces laid on a patch of mud. The boy came towards the woman in black and wailed, 'You shall die now!'

Ellie Booker (12)
Bradfield School, Sheffield

The Evil Man

The boy was running away from the evil man that was chasing him. Then he ran into an old castle. He went and hid in a cupboard and the man was shouting him. The man came closer to the boy. His heart was pumping as fast as a cheetah. Then, all of a sudden, the boy jumped out and ran into the fog. He could hear the man's footsteps. He went and hid behind a grave. Then he looked at it. It was his mum's grave. He started to run. He was very scared. He tripped over.

Kairan Taylor (12)
Bradfield School, Sheffield

The Figure

'Jess!' Tom shouted, as he stared down the endless narrow hallway of black abyss. He inched down the hallway and then there was a loud... scream. 'Jess!' Tom shouted, but there was no reply. Just the whistling of the wind. He started to stagger forwards until he reached a gravel oak door with a rusty handle and, as he put his hand on the bronze handle, a dark mysterious figure placed his hand on his back. 'Jess!' Tom trembled. But it wasn't Jess... 'Argh!'

Ryan Wilson (12)
Bradfield School, Sheffield

Grave

Stood in front of his grave, she tried making her scars from the accident discreet. 'I still love you!' Clouds lifted, sun lowered and a cold breath chilled her neck, hairs stuck up like soldiers on parade. Hesitantly she turned around. Looked down. Her shadow had vanished! The innocent lady's eyebrows instantly lowered. She edged back. Another breath. Behind her a black figure loomed. *Bang!* And there her grave was, next to her husband's.

The old widow's son travelled from afar to see his parents' graves. A cold breath chilled *his* neck… *Bang! Bang!*

Ellie Taylor (12)
Bradfield School, Sheffield

The Killer K9

Fog edged closer to her. She saw the grave. A tear trickled down her cheek, freezing in the winter breeze. A dog appeared, face as familiar as ice, smile as cold as snow. She backed away fearfully. Stumbling to the floor. *Bang!* The dog got closer. *Bang!* Her husband's grave stood in front of her. *Bang!* The dog's eyes turned red, desperately she tried to get to her feet. And then one final *bang!* There she was on the cold snow still as ice. Her eyes turned blood red, as she stumbled off into the eerie winter fog.

Kate Storey (12)
Bradfield School, Sheffield

Betrayed

Footsteps echo against paved ground. Skin tingles from the chill. Lips curve in a whistle, shaming those sleek, black crows. 'Fire is burning, don't let it catch you-ou.' Stone. Crumbling. Decaying. And somewhere underneath, a traitorous body. I remember the heat, recall the way those beautiful amber flames licked away at his body. Destroying him. Turning, I let the ebony parasol fall, and it bounces onto his grave. The scars are revealed; the painful gashes of fiery disfigurement are unleashed. I smile a small, mirthless smile. 'You know what they say dear, Hell hath no fury like a woman scorned.'

Anael Gillanders (13)
Bradfield School, Sheffield

What Lay Upstairs

I opened my eyes slowly. A dark limited room with only a door came to my vision. My body trembling I began to panic as I tried and failed to pull myself up from the dusty floorboards. My arms were above me, bound to something I couldn't quite name, my ankles somehow tied to the floor. I opened my mouth to scream, but a lifeless hand stopped me. I struggled frantically, but it was too late. A crimson flame rose above me and my eyes fluttered shut. She was the last thing I saw.

Charlotte Olivia Marie Butler (13)
Bradfield School, Sheffield

The Deadly Dungeon

It walked forward encouraging me to come in. 'Where are we going?' There was no reply from the thing in black. It opened the door, twisting the rusty knob, not showing its face, not once. Tentatively I stepped into the mysterious dungeon. *Slam!* The door shut behind me without anyone even touching it. The person or even thing turned towards me being extremely creepy like an owl. Just as I was going to see the face... a window smashed into pieces and the glass glided rapidly down to its head, it crashed to the floor.

Sasha Wynne (12)
Bradfield School, Sheffield

The Figure...

He walked along the misty, dark gravel pathway to his grandma's grave. As he approached, he could just about make out a female figure, a mere silhouette in the fog. He called out, 'Hello?' No answer. He started to walk closer, and saw the woman was holding a bouquet of roses. She stood unrealistically still. He put his hand gently on her shoulder and she slowly started to turn around. He took a few steps back. 'Grandma?' he asked.
Birds flew out of the trees as a short, sharp scream of pain erupted from the now empty graveyard.

Theo Cruddace (12)
Bradfield School, Sheffield

The Black Shadow

'We shouldn't go in there!' I whispered.
'Yes, but I need to get my ball back!' Tom shouted. It was there, stood in the mist.
'Hello?' I muttered. The lights started flickering. The floorboards creaking. Someone whispering in my ear.
'Run!' Tom screamed. It started following us, chasing us. The black shadow was there in the distance. Running out of the door through the bushes across the road, through the park.
'I think we have lost it,' I whispered.
'Yes, I think we have!'
I screamed.

Eva Brodrick (12)
Bradfield School, Sheffield

My Life Literally In My Hands

Walking through a church graveyard, mist rolls over haunted gravestones, I can tell something is going to happen. 'Hello, anyone?' No reply. Something is in the distance. The thing is coming closer and closer, coming faster and faster. I start running in the opposite direction, my heart is pounding. A tree in my sight waving its arms, so I climb as high as I can. But I fall. Thankfully I grasp onto a branch looking like it's going to snap. 'Help!' No one comes. And just as the ghastly monster goes away... *Snap!*

Joshua Peter Dyson
Bradfield School, Sheffield

Buried Alive

At my father's grave, my thoughts were interrupted by a muffled scream. I jumped back in terror. As my heart began to slow down, I stood up, mud and wood chippings hung onto the bottom of my dress. The scream. Could my dad still be alive? The curiosity was killing me inside. I frantically dug with my bare hands. All of a sudden the dirt began to crumble down both sides of the body. He sat up, grabbed my shoulders and pulled me to where he laid. A punch sent me dizzy. Suddenly, the dirt was getting pulled on me.

Ben Daley (13)
Bradfield School, Sheffield

Into The Fog

Fog gloomed around me and covered the sky. I couldn't see where I was going. Screams surrounded me as the snapping of twigs shook me as if someone was coming towards me. There were cries burying into my ears. It got louder, louder and louder. The fog was clearing up but was still hard to see. The sound of branches swaying from the treetops helped me notice where to go. The fog dimmed again and it seemed like the thickening fog was the night sky. Out of the corner of my eye, a dark figure approached, ready to get me...

Sean Wilson (12)
Bradfield School, Sheffield

The Mysterious Whisper

They are here. They have come for me. Is it too late? What is going to happen to me? They are coming closer towards me. Tall, dark figures with a sharp staff dripping with blood. I grab my phone out of my pocket and start calling my mum. There is no answer...
'Clara!' a voice whispers. 'Clara!' it whispered again. The tall dark figures are stood around me. *Poof!* They disappear. 'Clara!' I hear it again. I see another figure in the distance.
'Mum?' I mutter under my breath. *Bang!* It disappears. I feel something cold on my shoulder. 'Mum?'

Abigail Grace Jepson (12)
Bradfield School, Sheffield

Never Alone

I couldn't breathe. The light flickered and the rain smashed against the fragile windows. The hospital was cold but I knew I wasn't alone. I panicked as my phone vibrated. I didn't know the number, so ignored it. I found myself shaking as the hospital was abandoned. I looked up at the top of an old room, then looked down at my paper with the room number on. This was it. I peered around, the room was dark and had no sense of life. I saw her bony hands. A tear rolled down my face. 'Mum, is that you?'

Madeline Craft (12)
Bradfield School, Sheffield

Haunted House

I knocked on the door, it opened by itself. I walked in, a shiver ran down my spine. The floorboards creaked; I wasn't even walking... and then I saw it. It was a weird sort of shape. It moved closer to me. I screamed and ran off and tripped over a nail which was stuck in the floor. *Bang!* The door slammed behind me. What was it? Was I in danger? A candle flickered. Who lit it? Then that was it, the figure who I saw earlier grabbed me by my arm and dragged me through the door...

Molly Bramall (12)
Bradfield School, Sheffield

Witching Hour

It was dark. Moonlight shone in columns through the trees like torch beams. Fear pulsed through my veins. I wasn't alone. The faces of decrepit trees leered at me, sensing my vulnerability. Malevolent spirits taunted and laughed as I was enveloped in eerie sounds of scratching and howling; the eyes of the trees stared on. Gargantuan skeletons of branches prevented my escape like guards. The twelfth hour drew closer. A noise made me turn in surprise; I sliced my arm on a tree of knives. Three drops of blood fell. Far away, a tower struck twelve. Witching hour had begun.

Jodie Steer (13)
Bradfield School, Sheffield

-A

I'd been sat in the house all day. I decided to go to the graveyard to place some flowers at my friend's grave. She'd only been gone a year and we're still waiting to find out who killed her. As I got there it was pitch-black. Before I walked over I got a text, it was unknown, from someone called '-A' saying: 'Watch your back, danger is coming'. When I got to the grave it had been dug up, no flowers, no nothing. I was shocked. I ran as fast as a cheetah back to my car and left.

Meah Fox (13)
Bradfield School, Sheffield

The Forbidden Forest

I wander through the woods when I remember the strange happenings in these very trees... The rumours... The raindrops are like the tears of the clouds – the wind the screams of the victims who ventured these very woods. Startled, I turn back. But the path's gone... I'm lost... I'm trapped... Fog pours in. Surrounding me, seeping through the rocks, around the grass, towards the roots... towards... me. Thick mist engulfs me, and I am trapped within a heavy blanket of white. As it pours down my face, gushes down my throat, choking. I add my own screams to the wind...

Freya Foster (12)
Bradfield School, Sheffield

Eyes

In the dark I couldn't find the light switch, so I decided to brave it. My feet creaked the old wooden steps as I made my way down. At the bottom I thought I heard a noise. My heart started pounding. There it was again. A quiet, wasp-like noise. It was like it were crawling in my ear. I backed against the wall. Looking around I could hardly make out anything. I glanced back up the stairs. Then I looked properly. I saw two bright lights. But they weren't lights. They were eyes and they were looking straight at me.

Lydia Hindle (12)
Bradfield School, Sheffield

The Black

Why does it always hurt me? I'm always alone in this room and it kills me inside. I'm scared. Someone help me. Please before it gets me again and again. I'm struggling, about to die in blackness. He's coming! Light peers under the window. Relieved I am. But footsteps gradually get louder and bangs get louder in the corridors.. The noises stop and silence grows upon me. My life has come to an end, I can't do anything because I'm trapped here. No food in 24 hours. No water in 10 hours. I'm going to kill myself right now...

Joseph Patrickson (13)
Bradfield School, Sheffield

The Figure Of The School!

The figure stood there. John turned round. Screamed. Its face was as dark as the night. Its eyes were as red as blood. Sam whispered, 'What're we going to do?' The boys looked at each other. After a few moments they ran. Ran as far as they could. Suddenly, a scream came from behind. A ghost was standing there. A sad face with a torn, long, white dress. The ghost called them in but the boys tripped and found themselves lying breathless in a dark, lonely room. The school was haunted. Everything was silent.

Ciarra Chapman (12)
Bradfield School, Sheffield

The Black Figure

That night she walked down the hill through the woods, to the grave. Her face and skin pale like snow. Her clothes black, she held a bright but deep red rose. Walking up to the grave, she placed the red rose down gently, a tear fell.
All of a sudden, an ear-piercing scream echoed through the land. She quickly rose to her feet, then looked around. Her eyes piercing across the surrounding land. From the corner of one eye a black figure stood. A weird sort of object clutched in its hand, a bloodstained knife...

Holly Tingle (12)
Bradfield School, Sheffield

Haunted Prison Breaker

'Could it be?' Fluttering around the woods came a familiar person. A person who in the past was at one time the murdering head of the police department. He'd struck again, but in a different place. This time it was in the woods, completely out the ordinary? One of the two places he'd go to, or was it?
This story dates back to when the same person had trailed out more murders in the same prison. When he had an idea to blow up the prison and run away into the wood, which turned out being just a terrible dream...

Daniel Lee (12)
Bradfield School, Sheffield

Bite Marks

My eyes fluttered open, scanning the tiny dim room. For a moment I sat there staring into the shadows' emotionless faces. Why was I here? I tried to wrench myself upright, but my torso was pinned to the mouldy walls with a rope. Writhing free of its embrace, I lifted my arms, gasping. I stared down in disbelief. Gagging, I searched my arms, which were covered in bite marks. Mauve bruises surrounded them like a purple patchwork. I was a fly in a spider's trap, paralysed... A small girl-like figure scuttled up the ceiling towards me, whispering my name!

Sarah Westray (12)
Bradfield School, Sheffield

Vampires

'Tom!' I screamed as I ran down the stairs. 'Tom!' I was petrified. My pulse quickened as I ran through the decaying, old, eerie living room with the TV that makes that satanic crackling sound. I got to the door. It was locked. I tried to open the door. The door was old and there were blocks of light shooting through the glass. I scrambled upstairs to the bedroom. I could hear him slowly creeping up the stairs. The bedroom was full of hiding places. I heard the footsteps getting closer, and closer. I scrambled under the decaying bed... wailing...

Oliver Hallsworth (12)
Bradfield School, Sheffield

The Grave Of The Forgotten Soul

Fog crept around the crumbling tombstones, I wouldn't make it back before dawn. The moonlight performed dancing shadows over the graves of the dead. I drew in a deep, choking breath as I knelt before the decaying grave that sat all alone in the shadows. My hand was shaking... and not from the cold. Slivers of ice slid down my back as my fingers brushed the letters of the name I knew well. The name my mother gave me nearly 200 years ago. The name the grave bore. The grave which is never visited by a living soul. My grave...

Emma Kate Faxon (12)
Bradfield School, Sheffield

The Haunted Factory

I scrambled through the cracks in the old, abandoned, haunted factory in search of Oliver, my friend. *Bang!* A murder of crows flew from the old castle. 'Oliver!' I shouted. There was no reply, then suddenly mist covered the moon and started to descend into the dark, crumbling castle. Finally, I decided to go to the castle. I ran as fast as I could, but when I got there the door was smashed down. I ran towards where I heard the sound from Room 13! I thought it was the only one that was locked... Then, I shivered... and fell...

Sam Cottam (12)
Bradfield School, Sheffield

The Abandoned Chapel

I was walking back home, when it started to rain, it got very dark. I was getting soaked, so I ran into an abandoned chapel. The walls were tall and damp and it was very cold and gloomy inside. *Bang!* The door slammed shut behind me and I froze in terror. My phone rang. 'Where are you?' shouted Jim.
'I'm stuck inside an old, abandoned chapel,' I said.
'Well I'm on my way,' said Jim.
Then there was a knock on the door and, as I went to open it, a cold and gentle hand touched my back...

Oliver Davison (13)
Bradfield School, Sheffield

The Castle

My friend Jacob met me in the forest and we decided to go into an abandoned castle. The door was on the floor and the walls were decaying and collapsing. I shouted, 'Hello?' which made a massive echo. No reply. We carried on walking deeper and deeper into the dark tunnel. All of a sudden, *snap!* My friend had disappeared! He had fallen down a massive hole in the wood. I shouted down the hole, 'Are you OK?' No reply. I then felt a cold, arid, bony hand touch me. I was dragged backwards and there was... Dracula the vampire.

Jack Hunter Craine (12)
Bradfield School, Sheffield

Anne Curse

I stood there grieving. 'Why?' I whimpered. I looked down. Tears fell down my face, my ghostly white face. Fog weaved around the crumbling gravestone. My nightmares haunted me. A cold, spiky shiver ran down my back. The wind whistled. The moonlight cast dancing shadows over the ancient graveyard. 'Why? Why was I that person?' Dead flowers lay helplessly on the grave. I stood and stared. I listened to the screaming sounds of the crows. I unfroze my icy hands. Suddenly, a familiar figure appears. Flashbacks haunted me. I placed the flowers next to the name Anne Curse. That's me...

Emma Nicholson (13)
Bradfield School, Sheffield

The Shadow

The basement was dark. Cobwebs hung from the eroded ceiling. Rats scurried across the dusty floor. There was no light and my dim torch barely made things visible. I stood there silently looking around the cold, damp room. I heard a noise, it sounded like someone moving. I froze in horror and muttered nervously, 'Who's there?' but not a soul answered, they kept quiet. I got that feeling of someone watching me. I turned my head and noticed a shadow. An icy shiver ran down my spine, someone was watching me, but who was it?

Sarah Platts

Bradfield School, Sheffield

The Midnight Castle

It was midnight. Darkness surrounded me, I hadn't a clue where I was. Fog rose up from the ground. The owls were hooting and the wind howling. I carried on walking onwards and soon came across a haunting castle towering far above me, casting a huge forboding shadow upon me. Rain was pouring down and I desperately needed shelter so I went inside the castle... I looked around anxiously and saw a looming figure stood tall in front of me! I panicked, and ran for the door since I had thought that I was alone. But the door was locked...

Louis Edward Sutton (12)

Bradfield School, Sheffield

The Following

I was on my way back from school when a mist came in. I kept walking with a horrid feeling of someone following me. *Snap* went a twig. I looked behind and saw a black shadow of a person. I ran. I kept running with a cackling laugh following me. I must have hit my head. As I woke up in a graveyard surrounded by crows my head hurt. All of a sudden the crows flew off. I could see a woman in black walking down the eerie path. I blinked and she was gone, but a cackling laugh remained...

Alfie John Sutton (12)
Bradfield School, Sheffield

The Forest Tribe

I walked along the rotting path. It was dark, very dark. The wind blew in my ears. 'Is someone there?' I shouted. 'Jake, stop playing tricks!' I whimpered. There was no reply. The leaves rustled. I started to run, I got as far away as possible. I sat behind a tree in the never-ending forest. Devil-like eyes glared at me but before I knew it, I was knocked out cold.
I woke up to see what almost looks like a tribal ceremony and I was their sacrifice. They chanted in a different language. 'Run, before it's too late!'

Ellie Petch (12)
Bradfield School, Sheffield

The Deadly Graveyard

She drifted slowly between the crumbling gravestones. Her deadly black wedding dress flowed behind her as she crept, glancing at the terrible darkness while holding blood-red roses. Unanticipatedly, she saw her husband's gravestone shadowing through the misty fog. She crouched down and laid the murderous roses on the dirty stone. The moonlight cast a black shadow behind her. The tall trees swayed as her charcoal hair dropped as she got up. Then, suddenly, the atmosphere went silent like death. She felt a bitter cold hand touch her shoulder, and she turned around in trepidation. Nothing was there...

Charlotte Bladen
Bradfield School, Sheffield

Angels And Demons!

The dark figure stood at the bottom of the stairs looking up at me like a tiger would look at their prey. 'Mum, Dad?' Nobody answered. It was deadly silent until screaming voices, whispering voices, and cackling laughs were sounded in my head. The door slammed open, as a gust of wild wind blew vigorously. My heart suddenly quickened, as I felt someone's cold breath on the back of my neck. But how? The silhouette was at the bottom of the stairs. There must have been someone else. Someone else beside me. *Boom!* The candles went out. Suddenly, darkness fell...

Sophie Webster (12)
Bradfield School, Sheffield

The Cellar

As I crept into the cellar a powerful stench hit my nose. I looked into one of the vats and saw human heads. As I looked into the next vat I saw something worse, human brains. The very sight of one made me feel sick, but around 50 was too much. As I looked to the very end of the cellar, I saw a very large stack of torsos, all of them had no heads and a hole in the middle of the body where the heart should be. 'Hello, are you looking for something?' echoed a high, cold voice.

Alex White (12)
Bradfield School, Sheffield

Walking Alone

A bone-chilling scream broke the silence of the night. *What was that?* I thought. 'I should have stayed at the party,' I murmured. Satanic laughing from ahead sent shivers down my spine. I decided to call Sarah to come and pick me up. *Bleep!* Out of charge. My phone was at 72% before I left the party. Another scream echoed down the empty street but this time it was right behind me...I stopped and willed myself to turn around. Nothing there. Nothing but a shadow. However, the more I looked, I realised that this unexplained shadow wasn't mine.

Emilia Crawley (12)
Bradfield School, Sheffield

Graveyard

There was an abandoned graveyard across the road from where I lived. On Halloween we went into it. Everyone said it was haunted. I had been in there for an hour and I could see a picture that had been set on fire on top of a grave. It was a picture of me on my dad's grave and my picture had a red cross through my face. I could feel someone behind me grabbing my clothes, and touching my neck. It stopped. Then it started again later on. I turned around. It was my dad. But he was dead...

Charlotte Lister (13)
Bradfield School, Sheffield

The Haunted Girl

I didn't know it was true. I thought it was just a story... I was walking home from the club with fog blinding me, whispers filled the air. 'Is anybody there?' I murmured, the fog slowly lifted to show a path leading to a church with smashed windows. The door creaked open. I felt something inching me forward to it, when I looked around nobody was there. Suddenly, I saw a figure staring at me through the window. I blinked and it had gone. I shuffled to the door, cautious of what would come next. Then, the door slammed shut...

Lauren Bailey (13)
Bradfield School, Sheffield

A Mysterious Figure In The Distance

A cold shiver went down my spine as I saw the abandoned castle. *I will go and wait until the rain stops and then I will head home,* I thought. The fog started to creep closer and closer. I crept down by a tree to try and shelter from the pouring rain. But, suddenly, I sensed someone was following me! 'Hello?' I called, as I tried to look through the pouring rain but only the sound of a heart beating was heard. *Bang!* A tree came crashing down as a tall, dark figure appeared in the distance. I gulped.

Emilia Lucy Graham (12)
Bradfield School, Sheffield

The Gargoyles

I inched down the gravelled path with the sound of crunching stones loud in my ears. All around me naked branches reached out like feverish beggars seeking attention. The neglected archways of what once was a beautiful church reared before me like a long forgotten gateway to Hell. The merciless rain stabbed onto my exposed chilled skin like thousands of assassins' knives. I reached the deserted and crumbling graves and screamed as from out of the corner of my eye ancient gargoyles jumped at me with malicious eyes, their demonic pitch-black lips curling at the corners, rising into rictus grins!

Eva Husband (12)
Bradfield School, Sheffield

The Cold Hand!

Fog walked over the dark old castle. I wouldn't be home before darkness. I saw something lurking in the corner of my eye. I stumbled across the crooked path. I quickly got my phone, it was missing! As I walked up to the old, abandoned castle, I tried to open the old, rusty, wooden door. It was unlocked. It was dark inside. I felt like something was behind me. I turned as fast as I could. Nothing was there. I sat down and started to cry. Something touched me on my bad shoulder, the hand was as cold as ice.

Jessica Doyle
Bradfield School, Sheffield

It

He could sense what was coming when he walked in. It was here he felt it, death. Good old painful death was here. He wasn't afraid, he knew it was over. It was there lurking in dark places, creeping and searching for him. Kill the richest man in the valley who was an ex-marine. It didn't like these facts, it couldn't care less that his wife and kids would be discombobulated by the events. First it went for his jugular, ripping it out, sending blood everywhere. Next his stomach was in the cross hairs...

Dan Worth
Bradfield School, Sheffield

The Creature In The Basement

I enter the basement. There's nothing there, just dust and dirt. I turn on the light. There's only one bulb, therefore it doesn't help. I look around, searching for something that will be helpful, only to find a door with scratches and marks engraved in the wood. I try the rusty handle. It is hard to open. I have to barge into it with my shoulder. I look around the room, it is pitch-black, it takes me a while to see. The smell is terrible. I look up to see a large figure over me, staring right at me...

Elliott Newhall (12)
Bradfield School, Sheffield

The Devil Dog And The Girl

As I was walking back to where the cameramen were waiting to take me home, I heard a scream through the darkness. Quickly, I ran to the clearing. Wait... where was everyone? Then I saw the car, a bolt of lightning shot down my back. On the side of the car were four long, sinister-looking claw marks. Blood was everywhere... I needed to get out of here, how could a wonderful day turn so suddenly into this? I was petrified. I wrapped my coat tightly around me and looked around to check I wasn't dreaming. No, this was real...

Emma Maisy Thompson (13)
Bradfield School, Sheffield

The Rising Dracula

It was midnight, my dad had left me home alone while he was at the pub drinking pints of beer. He did this every night since Mother had died. Usually when my dad went out, I would go to my mummy's grave. I had decided to go now. As I opened the door I saw the storm, it was getting worse, so I ran. Now I had reached the most dark and gloomy graveyard in the world. There was not one spot of colour about this place. Suddenly, this creature raised up from the dead earth. 'Argh Dracula. Argh! Argh!'

Daisy Leahy (12)
Bradfield School, Sheffield

Shadows Of The Graveyard

Snow covered the ground like a blanket, and darkness greeted me. I walked up to my father's grave. My heart ached. *One year today,* I thought. In the darkness, I made out shadows behind the largest grave of them all. Walking cautiously, I placed the wilting flowers with my father and stumbled to see more. Frost covered the isolated grave, I wiped it away. 'Death of Rose Smithe'. Underneath the crumbled writing was a picture of... me. 'What? It can't be?' I whispered. Screams pierced my ears, something pushed down on my back, clawing me further deep underground, suffocating me.

Mia Heeley (13)
Bradfield School, Sheffield

The Graveyard

Carefully the two mischievous boys climbed over the rusty steel gate, into the graveyard. Running quickly one of the trouble-making boys tripped over an ancient stone grave and engraved into the stone read a message saying: 'Do not disturb or suffer the consequences!'
So, being the horrible little boys they are, both of them decided to jump up and down on the grave. Then, suddenly, rising from the ground a pale white ghost screamed, so loud it would break a glass. Trembling, the two boys looked at each other nervously, while they both loudly shouted, 'Run!' Did they get away...?

Oliver George Glover (13)
Bradfield School, Sheffield

Tombstone Terror

The wind picked up, the air got colder, it was not a good night to come here. I trudged along the pitch-black, musty walkway, all alone and out of sight. I stumbled upon a jagged stone and came face-to-face with the most mysterious tombstone I had ever spotted. I scraped my finger across the moss-covered rubble. 'David Ghouler' read the top of the plaque. 'I know that name from somewhere!' I murmured in the gloomy air.
'Looking for me?' a voice cackled from behind me. As I turned around, I hesitated, and took a deep breath...

Joseph Smith (13)
Bradfield School, Sheffield

Darkness

I ran... this place is too gloomy, too isolated to be safe. The darkness swallowed me up like a gaping black hole, twisting and turning, ripping all of the happiness out of my heart. An icy-cold hand clamped its fingers into an iron strong grip around my shoulder. Turning swiftly I screamed. Cold as ice, he stood alone in the darkness. Glazed over with the painful memory of his past, his pale eyes seemed to bore their way into my soul. I was frozen to the spot. One word exploded like a bomb going off inside my mind... Vampire!

Olivia Fothergill (12)
Bradfield School, Sheffield

Danger!

I knew I should've listened to Mum! She told me never to go into the forbidden wood. I didn't listen. Something started stalking. I ran! I was running so fast my poor lungs were burning. The ebony coloured trees whizzed past me. 'It' didn't stop. 'Don't stop, don't stop, don't stop,' I murmured to myself. The darkness made no difference to the speed that I ran. On the floor flesh lay rotting, making the forest reek of dead nails. A pain started in my neck! It felt like I had been struck by lightning! 'Help me!'

Rowan Flewitt (13)
Bradfield School, Sheffield

Nightmare Shift

He felt like the unluckiest man in the world. As Michael drove up to the house, he felt a little pinch in his heart. Once he got there, he entered the dead, silent house. Then he walked up to the bedroom, where he was told to set up shop. As he walked into the room he sat down and grabbed his flashlight.

Two hours passed and nothing happened. Then, suddenly, he heard something come from outside. He opened the left door and used his flashlight to see who was there. It was something he couldn't even describe. 'Oh God, help...!'

Oliver Hurst (12)
Bradfield School, Sheffield

Maddison Avenue

The sky crackled with laughter as the clouds opened. The rain hit my head. I broke into a sprint. Faster and faster, corner after corner, I ran. The van squealed as it followed. The bright skyscrapers that lined Maddison Avenue flashed in the corner of my eye. Shouting voices echoed in my ears. I rapidly ran across the avenue and slipped down an alleyway. *Oh no*, I thought as a brick wall came into sight. My head swivelled round to look for a way out... There wasn't one! The van's engine roared behind me. What was I going to do?

Eleanor Brook (12)
Bradfield School, Sheffield

The Door To Nowhere

There was an old door in our garden wall. It didn't go anywhere, but there was a key. Everyone said it didn't go anywhere. So why was there a key?

One day, it was raining. I was bored so I went to find the key. I took the key and went to the door. The key turned in the rusty lock. *Creak!* That was the door. Behind it was blackness. No wall, just black, so I found a torch and went inside. *Bang!* The door closed. I jumped. My torch flickered and went out. *Thump!* What was that? *Thump! Thump...!*

Molly Miranda Norton (13)
Bradfield School, Sheffield

Into The Vault

I was walking down the cold, wet stairs, it was dark. There were anti-depressant pills everywhere, I looked for the doctor's office, still quietness and too much of it, then... *bang,* right in front of me! I started to run, then I hit a guy, except he wasn't a human he was a mutant.

'Argh! Human!' he hissed.

I was running until I hit the wall of a child's bedroom. 'Human!' 'Argh!'

There were dolls everywhere looking at me. I hid under a rocky chair next to me – a child's corpse. Something grabbed my leg... The corpse, I screamed!

Jacob Baxter (12)
Bradfield School, Sheffield

Hell's Shack

Thunder echoed through the moonlit skies as the storm closed on Jack. 'Where can I find shelter?' he asked himself multiple times. The only place left that wasn't submerged in a river of water was, as local kids called it, Hell's Shack. What were his options? You didn't want to get caught in a storm like this! He knelt down and covered his head, only to feel safe. The pounding rain on the wooden planks above sounded like a monster's quaking footsteps, but soon they were too loud. He squirmed around in the dusty cobwebs as the door creaked open.

James Andrew Webb (12)
Bradfield School, Sheffield

The Storm

We were walking in snow. Very deep snow. 'It's cold.'
'Bronte, is that all you're worried about?' I almost screamed.
'Sorry, I was just breaking the silence!'
I stopped in my tracks. What is that? Please don't be that, please. I touched it. Bronte just stood staring. It was definitely blood. I gulped. 'We should go.' The snow was getting worse.
'Yeah,' I said in reply. We turned around. *Scream!* I felt a sharp pain in my leg, I fell to floor, the black-hooded guy staring at me. I looked at my leg. It was all red. Oh no...

Abigail Jones (12)
Bradfield School, Sheffield

Mr Creek

Slowly my soft fingers met with the angelic doll's house I had stumbled upon in the mysterious house. *Creak!* Mesmerised, I opened the door and discovered a note… Intrigued, I read it: 'Don't move a muscle, don't even speak, he watches closely, he's Mr Creek!' Terrified, I wanted to run, but my feet were fused to the floor, so I searched for another: 'He's watching now, he's in the room if you dare to look you'll see him soon!' A petrified tear escaped my eye, I examined the last note to myself; my head turned to the ceiling. *Scream! Creak…*

Lucy Barker (13)
Bradfield School, Sheffield

A Christmas Bang

It was Christmas Eve, the records were playing, the presents were wrapped. Finally, a Christmas with no anger; just smiles. 'Esmae… Esmae darling, can you do me a favour and take this to Cliff across the road?' my mother called me, passing over a hamper full of basic things, anybody should have on Christmas Day.
So off I went out the door, it was a gorgeous snowy night, the lights were on, the trees were up. I knocked on his door but there was no answer, I stepped inside shouting his name.
'Hello, dearie,' a voice spoke… 'Goodbye, dearie.' *Bang!*

Ellie Scott-Brown (12)
Bradfield School, Sheffield

The Grave

Suddenly, I woke up. Something felt different. I walked down the stairs and looked out of the window, it was dark and raining. There was someone out there but it was too dark to see. I opened the door slowly. There was a tall, skinny man, he looked at me with lifeless eyes. His face was green and he wore ragged clothes. He beckoned me forward with his bony fingers. Frightened, I followed him. We walked for over an hour until we reached an old grave, he pointed at it, with a frown. It was my name... I was dead.

Grace Ellie Hickson-Shaw (12)
Bradfield School, Sheffield

I Recognised His Face

Darkness spread through the city. Out of the corner of my eye, I saw a blur of light. Falling to the floor, I gasped. The cold rain trickled down my back. I quickly crawled along the wet, muddy floor and hid behind a gravestone. Minutes passed as I waited for the right time to run. 'Three, two, one.' I charged forward but hurled myself back as a distorted figure stepped into the light. A cold shiver ran through my spine. I felt sick, I recognised his face. Suddenly, a stabbing pain hit my stomach; I fell to the cold floor.

Milly Bentley
Bradfield School, Sheffield

The Discovery

'Hello? Who's there?' *Drip... Drip... Drip...* I slowly inched towards where the noise was coming from. Each room was perfectly tidy. One bed, one wardrobe, no window. I edged along the seemingly never-ending corridor.

Eventually I reached the room where the sound was coming from. I twisted the lock tentatively. Locked. I peeped through the obsidian keyhole. It was obviously inhabited. Bed sheets were sprawled across the floor, a lamp flickered in the corner, a wardrobe was swinging open. As I glanced around I noticed where the dripping noise was coming from... He was hanging from the ceiling...

Molly Isobel Parkin (13)
Bradfield School, Sheffield

Tears Of Blood

I could hear the flutter of a bat's wings behind me. My heart was beating faster and faster with every step I took. What was I even doing? The swaying branches cast horrifying shadows by my feet, following me everywhere I went. Picking up the pace, I started running, desperately wanting to get out of the trap I stupidly let myself into. *Bang!* Oh no! She had found me, at long, long last. I didn't have long. *Bang!* Louder this time. She was getting closer. *Bang!* There she was, right in front of me. Screaming. Crying. Crying tears of blood...

Brontë Ruth Pendleton (13)
Bradfield School, Sheffield

Death Will Come To All

Who was it? What was it? What did it want? What are we going to do? I thought. It was kill or be killed, but how could we kill it? No one knew what it was or how it came into existence, but if we didn't act fast we would die. This... thing was going to kill us, but it seemed that it stuck to the shadows like a ghost. Waiting for the right time to strike. We had to find a weakness to kill it, or distract it long enough to escape... or death will come to all.

Oliver Frow
Bradfield School, Sheffield

Lost

I was totally lost. In the deep, dark forest, on a cold night, I was terrified. I heard a sudden noise, my knees buckled weak, I started to run. Fast. My heart pounding like a tiger's heavy paws hitting the ground. My mind went into isolation, I didn't know what to do. So I hid. I found shelter in a nearby, desolated shed. But the noise was still there, closer than ever before. And louder. The door was suddenly broken down. It was time to find out what was there, was it anything? Was I paranoid and just imagining it?

Oliver Thomas Graham (12)
Bradfield School, Sheffield

As The Crows Fled

As the crows flew and the river shimmered in the moonlight, even the crows had abandoned me, and it seemed only I didn't know what was happening. A voice came, but who knows where from. 'She only comes out at 12am.' But who came out at 12am? I could see a shadow out of the corner of my eye, but I was so gripped by fear I could not turn. Her cold breath tingled down my neck, and her scent was too strong to bear. Her hand slowly crept onto my shoulder. I tried running, but it was too late.

Jessica Crossland
Bradfield School, Sheffield

The Dark House

The old house was pitch-black. Doors were opening and shutting. Cobwebs were everywhere. Spiders running out of the house, there was a weird sound coming from upstairs, a smell I'd never smelt before. I started walking upstairs to see if I could see anything. I went in this room. I walked up to a bookcase. I looked into a mirror and there was this little girl. I turned around and nothing was there. I ran downstairs and the smell became stronger, the girl was there again. I ran out of the house screaming and shouting, 'Help me!'

Courtney Rebecca Louise Rodgerson (13)
Bradfield School, Sheffield

Spooky Thing

One day there was a spooky person. He was hiding in the bushes. He wouldn't come out of the bushes.

The next day people came to live in the cottage that was near the bushes. The people saw the spooky person. The police were looking around. The policeman knocked on the cottage door, but it was not the policeman, it was the spooky person from hiding in the bushes. They shut the door and screamed. The policeman got the spooky person and he killed him. He was chopped to pieces. He was dead.

Jamie Needham (12)

Bradfield School, Sheffield

After The Relatives Left

After her relatives left the funeral, Anna stood alone in the damp graveyard, her short matted hair falling just past her shoulders. The long winding path through the stone-filled field held nothing but secrets. Whispers darted around, reflections of the dead flickered and kept catching her eye. A cold sigh of wind scattered a few rustling leaves beneath her feet. The church bell struck two, startling three crows that were chatting in the treetops. She took a deep breath and began to make her way out of the empty yard when a firm grip grabbed hold of her right shoulder...

Eleanor Jane Charlesworth (13)

Bradfield School, Sheffield

I See You

There it was, a crumbling monument. I crept closer as the fog snaked its way past me. There was a massive crumbling doorway, the doors were open. Someone had been here recently, someone was over there, who could it be? The hooded person walked forward and got closer and closer. The person pulled down their hood and shouted, 'Are you ready to suffer?' As a gust of wind came in with a billow of fog, then they disappeared. I slowly walked forward and then there was a scream, where did it come from? The tower!

Alex Capener (12)
Bradfield School, Sheffield

Where?

Blood, everywhere. We knew of them. One of them tricked me. It stood, smiling, eyes swirling. My feet were rooted to the ground. Why couldn't I move? 'Hello Poppet!' it greeted me. That wasn't my brother. Yet it was at the same time. Our parents lay on the floor covered in a thick crimson liquid. Finally, my legs let me run. It was too late. I was knocked unconscious. I don't know how long I was knocked out for, but when I woke everything was in chaos. The black room spun as the scent of war hit my nose.

Harriet Gray (12)
Bradfield School, Sheffield

Attack Of The Crows

My heart sounded like a machine gun in a battle. A wall of crows entangled me in a web of fear. I started running. I called out for help but my voice was drowned out by the piercing screams of crows. The crows chased, pulling at my clothes violently. Even with hundreds of crows on my tail I felt alone for no one in the world knew I needed help. The castle hemmed me in, there was nowhere to go. Why were they so determined to catch me? Who had sent them to catch and kill me?

Aidan Berry (12)
Bradfield School, Sheffield

Scattered Thoughts

Bang...! The rumbling sounds of incoming death resonated throughout the place. We heard the thunderous thud of bombs rattling the shallow pits, followed quickly by the snap of door hinges and the ceaseless roar of enemy voices, bullets and the heart-rending cries of those who were taking their final breath.
A bell tolled loudly in the background, distracting me from my scattered thoughts and resealing the wounds of my scarred memories. I glanced around to see people, their faces soon moulding into the enemies slaughtered. That's what I remember of November 11. What do you remember this November?

Katie Yarrow (14)
Brinsworth Academy, Rotherham

We Are Alone

Blood dripped from a pale young hand onto the decayed railing like an avalanche of pure red. A lone girl was limping up a dark, depressed staircase, laced with red sticky liquid and a decomposing corpse of mangled lives. Her eyes leaked of darkness, slipping down her cheeks, becoming more intense with each trembling step. Echoes surrounded her like screeching snake reflecting off the wretched windows, shattered glass and pulverised promises. Steps shattered beneath the girl, swinging her backwards at a bullet's beat. Long, lifeless hair flew behind, revealing scars, scratches and slashes. Silence hung like that of mist.

Thomas Peck (14)
Brinsworth Academy, Rotherham

The Unknown

From behind her, Casey heard the door of the barn creak open. She froze... her feet appeared to glue to the hay-covered floor as a huge gush of icy wind sent goosebumps dancing up her arms.
Three eerie footsteps approached her direction. 'Who's there?' she called, as her heart pounded out of her chest. There was no reply... A dark shadow lured and, with every moment, it grew larger and larger until she was submerged into complete darkness. Shivers tiptoed down Casey's spine as a cool breath spread across the back of her neck.

Megan Jade Fuller (15)
Brinsworth Academy, Rotherham

Just A Dream...?

Max lies half asleep, unsettled, when the door creaks open. Peeking through one eye, a dark crooked-like figure leans on his door, holding the dead bodies of Max's mother and father. Max takes a deep breath, squeezing his eyes shut, not moving an inch.

Movement. The figure shuffles forward towards Max's bed, propping the bodies onto nearby chairs. Using the corpses' blood he writes a message on the wall then crawls under Max's bed.

An hour passes. While Max's eyes adjust to the terrifying darkness he is able to peer over and read the message: 'I know you're awake!'

Maddie Daniels Smith (15)

Brinsworth Academy, Rotherham

The Night Before The Nightmare

There I lay. I can't move! I can't even open my eyes. Unable to move, I can feel the sharp shards of glass puncturing my delicate skin The screams are getting louder as the ringing in my ears fades away. *Bang!* Again I hear the sound of a gun, I occasionally feel a warm heat blow upon my face. Eventually my eyes regain sight; however the bitter darkness haunts me. Suddenly, a cold, bloody hand covers my mouth and nose, as a sharp object is pressed into the side of my head. I hear a trigger being pulled. Goodbye me?

Holly Bennett (13)

Brinsworth Academy, Rotherham

Diary Of A Soldier

Shells were dropping everywhere. Thousands of young soldiers were just lying there – dead. Amongst them I could see my brother, Freddie. He looked awful, from a fit, young boy to a frail old body. I saw everyone else, just the same. Me and a few others were left and we had to fight – no matter what the consequences. For King and country. We charged, dodging every bullet that came firing at us. It was great! Suddenly, without warning, a shell dropped and wounded me. Despite this, I tried to follow my crew but I didn't have the strength to move.

Hafsa Mirza (11)
Brinsworth Academy, Rotherham

The Blackout

A blackout, for what seemed like forever finally gave way. He made his way up, however it seemed impossible. He glanced down to see blood on his injured hands and legs. However, under all the blood were straps, tightened around his wrists. He screamed loudly, and wailed for his life, eventually a tall, black figure stomped towards him, then stood... He slowly turned, to see it. A gigantic, destructive hammer. He froze. He felt scared. The death stick swung. Having fast reflexes, he ducked. He was relieved, surely he had avoided his death. However, the hammer swung again...

Zak Martin (12)
Crofton Academy, Wakefield

The Lullaby

I held my breath as I walked silently along the corridor. I saw the door. *Thud!* I froze. Something was behind me. Turning my head slowly I forced my eyes to look back at the corridor. There was nothing there. I turned back to the door. I reached out and held the cold metal doorknob. Gritting my teeth I twisted the doorknob. It opened. Light burst out of the room. Covering my eyes I saw there was a music box staring at me. I felt drawn to it. Suddenly, the door slammed shut. The music box started playing a lullaby.

Ella Allen (12)

Crofton Academy, Wakefield

The Cabin

The dark mist filled my lungs. It was hard to breathe but I couldn't go back, not yet. As the branches pulled and ripped my clothes, as if they were alive and needed something, the darkness crept across the starless night. *Crash!* It was close. *What do I do?* was my only thought. *What do I do?* The cabin! Yes the cabin. I could see it now: the birch wood cabin. *Snap!* I could almost feel its warm black breath slither into my body and corrupt me. I was there, just one more...

Dylan Fordyce (12)

Crofton Academy, Wakefield

Dark, Dull Day In The Cellar

I awoke surprisingly stuck in a dark cellar in what seemed the middle of nowhere. I was constantly hearing unexplained noises coming from the distance. My heart was racing quicker than a Lamborghini, at top speed. I was searching for light left, right and centre, but saw no signs. The footsteps were starting to get closer and closer, as my heartbeat was getting faster and faster. The footsteps were point blank. All of a sudden lights came on. I witnessed a group of men holding baseball bats. Suddenly, I saw one of them swing for me...

Shane Kirton (12)
Crofton Academy, Wakefield

The Bloody Path

A group of friends were walking through an empty field late at night, they came across something dodgy, an illuminated blood path telling them to follow it. If they did they wouldn't return but if they didn't then they would die! They stopped and stared, scared not knowing what to do. Deathly silent. After what seemed like a lifetime, they decided to follow the path. A few minutes later they heard a whistle, it became closer and closer and then suddenly... nothing but silence. Then a ghostly whisper, 'Do not take one more step!' But they did...

Bree Adlington (12)
Crofton Academy, Wakefield

Untitled

One day, Jim and Jeff went out to the Floating Table Diner. On their way they realised that no one was on the streets, so they went to their friend's house. He and his girlfriend had turned into zombies and when they ran to the door and stepped outside, everyone else had turned into zombies. They had to sprint home and get their ray guns and blast everyone to cure them. But, as they got to the door, there were zombies blocking them in.

Tyler Mason (12)
Crofton Academy, Wakefield

The Night

It was freezing. I pulled the covers over my mouth and nose to try to keep warm. My eyes glared wide open into the pitch-black darkness of the room. I could see nothing. I felt as if my heart was going to jump out of my chest. All that I could hear was *thud, thud, thud!* The shouting from next door had got louder all night. They'd just moved in. People say their children disappeared, and were never found. Shouting had turned to silence. I was relieved. I was finally drifting to sleep… *Bang, bang, bang!* I sprang up.

Joel Healey (12)
Crofton Academy, Wakefield

Untitled

It was a cold, windy, terrifying night by the haunted mansion, in Yorkshire. I walked past it every day on the way back from school and today was the day I was going to enter. Prepared with a torch I walked up the path to the nightmare abandoned mansion. I felt cold and ill but at the same time excited and curious. I opened the old, wooden, rickety door. I walked in, looked around and found a door with the sign: *No Entry!* I entered and, at the first step, I felt a big, strong hand touch my shoulder...

Yorck Newrick (13)

Crofton Academy, Wakefield

The Drive

As the car came to a halt, Gary felt worried. He checked his phone but there was no signal. He waited for hours but no vehicles passed. He sat looking into the moonlit woods. He noticed lights coming from a building. He walked towards it. Gary could hear all different sounds from around the woods. He heard a cry which startled him. Gary froze and looked around. He started walking towards the building. Gary noticed a large hole in the ground, it was a grave. Then he felt a cold, clammy hand on his shoulder. He screamed.

Lewis Nixon (12)

Crofton Academy, Wakefield

Walking Grave

I ran and ran. The wind whistled, louder and louder, faster and faster.
A bolt of lightning struck from behind setting the midnight sky alight.
I flew through the gates. I knew I had to be quick if I wanted to make
it out alive. 'Devil's place', that is what my dad always used to say.
My dad isn't a devil, it was the Devil that killed him. As I arrived at the
half broken gravestone, I heard that someone was calling me. Had
someone followed me? It wasn't someone, no it can't be, maybe no,
please… 'Argh…!'

Emily Gallivan (12)

Crofton Academy, Wakefield

Black Figure

'Where am I?' the man questioned himself. 'All I can remember is a
bright, white light and a mysterious, black shadow.' He was laid in a
dark, grey room surrounded by nothing but a rotting corpse with all
its guts missing. *Roar!* 'What was that?' The door suddenly started
to rise. The mysterious figure stood before him and roared. The man
stood up and ran. He could hear deep breaths. He stopped, it was a
dead end. There was nothing else to do. He leant up against the wall
and waited. The black figure appeared for the last time.

Jack Price (12)

Crofton Academy, Wakefield

The Corner Is Where He Hides

My bloodshot eyes dart across the room as trees whistle, almost whispering my name. The full moon casting dancing shadows through dusty windows. Tears pricking my eyes, threatening to spill as the noises get louder and I hear them closing in. I'm doomed as the hatch slowly opens. All I see is a hand covered in blood as I shuffle backwards. Then I see it, a face with no features, just empty black sockets dripping with a metallic substance. He simply stares at me like we're in a staring contest. That's the last thing I see. Him in the corner!

Kirsty Yare (13)
Crofton Academy, Wakefield

The Cottage

It was dusk. The wind howled and the rain was like daggers hitting his face. He walked through the trees. Ahead he could see a derelict cottage, in the distance. A dog yapped and a blood moon was rising. He was drawn to the cottage like metal attracted to a magnet. The hinges wailed as he pushed open the door and the floorboards creaked. He had an eerie feeling of someone watching him. The atmosphere was dark and foreboding. Under the stairs was a door, as he reached it there was a blood-curdling scream and something touched his shoulder...

Lucy Harrison (12)
Crofton Academy, Wakefield

Graveyard

It was midnight. The shiny, white moon was overhead. Sindy was walking through the graveyard. Suddenly, she heard footsteps behind her. She turned around quickly. Nothing. No one was there. She turned back around. Slightly scared, but carried on walking. About 20 seconds later she felt something touch her on her arm. She gasped and stopped. She started to run as fast as she could. The air started to get cold but it was summer. When she got home her parents walked over and said that her grandma had just died. She started crying but then remembered about the graveyard.

Samantha Morris (13)
Crofton Academy, Wakefield

The Elusive Spider

'Oh my, not again!' squawked Chris, as he saw yet another cobweb glistening in the moonlight. 'I'm catching this spider if it's the last thing I do!' he exclaimed. No matter how many times Chris tried to catch the spider, it always eluded him. With every waking day that passed, more and more cobwebs formed, until Chris found himself trapped inside his own home. Every window and door was plagued with thick, dense layers of cobwebs, hanging like tangles of ancient hair, white, dirty and tangled, with everyone thinking the house was abandoned. Chris has to tackle the nightmare alone.

Qaim Khan (12)
Crofton Academy, Wakefield

Krampus: A Christmas Horror Story – Part 1

One snowy night the Frazers had so much fun on Christmas Eve. They played board games but their son Owen found two horrible, terrifying Christmas statues. That were Krampus and Santa. However, Owen accidently knocked Santa off the window and broke it. He found a note in it. It had blood on it.

One day later Owen heard a noise on the roof saying, 'You're going to get grappled by my long, slimy tongue.' *Bang!* went the chimney. He got a knife from the kitchen. He touched Santa but it was Krampus. Owen stabbed him. It took him to Hell…

Owen Brown (11)

Darton College, Barnsley

Death By Knife

Life was getting strange for Nathan. He was getting old. He was married to Kacey, but he was getting tired of her – he planned to do something gruesome. He planned to murder her – not thinking twice! Meanwhile, Kacey was unsure of how Nathan was feeling; he seemed to be getting ill. *Tonight*, Nathan thought, *tonight I shall kill my wife.* He edged forward, grabbing his knife. 'Kacey, come on!' He stabbed her, the smell of blood made him excited.

Two days later, Nathan felt scared, 'The body, oh the body!' He felt nervous and killed himself in a house fire!

Kacey Anne McNicholas (11)

Darton College, Barnsley

Curse Of The Dead

'You're going to kill those slopes!' I shook my head back and forth, staring at the 100ft drop below. Among the mountains, behold a storm. Gusts of wind shook the ski-lift pushing me forward. My breathing increased. My body was now at its limit, muscles screaming; glands unable to produce adrenaline. The next second, all I remembered was waking up to my heart beating. Rain began to fall. I ran. My legs, exhausted, but I ran. I discovered a cave, warmer than outside. A blink startled me. 'Run!' whispered a voice. A knife impaled me evacuating blood. My heart stopped.

Poppy Caunt (11)

Darton College, Barnsley

Life Or Death

It was a dark, gloomy night in November when a man and his family were killed and nobody knew who did it. When someone found out the killer was a young, troubled youth, who didn't know the meaning of life, he decided to take it away from others who had the feeling. Six families were slaughtered in their houses until the youngster was caught and sent to death. He managed to escape, he took an innocent, vulnerable child hostage. The pair were never seen again. Looking out of a grimy, dirty window a silhouette of a vague character stood looking.

Thomas Downend (12)

Darton College, Barnsley

Killing Revenge

Sally stumbled into the room and handed Trevor a cup of tea, there was mist on the walls. The trees swayed with the wind's breath, and rain pattered onto the foggy windows. Trevor bounced upstairs. Sally followed him, she rushed into their room and opened the oak dresser. Inside was his journal, continuously on the pages were pictures of him and a woman, and with a red marker was a cross drawn on her. Sally realised that Trevor was the killer going round. Before she could do anything, Trevor sneaked behind her and said, 'Too late!' and Sally had gone...

Ellie-Jo Bradley (11)
Darton College, Barnsley

The Haunted Lullaby

One lullaby, one girl, hundreds of dolls... A scratch on the door, she woke to nothing but the doll! Footsteps on the floorboards she woke, but didn't rise. A tap on the shoulder, she woke only to see the doll that laid next to her. As she fell asleep, she heard a voice, 'Once a dream, once a curse, once again I'll never leave.'
'Argh!' she screamed. Her mum and dad raced to see! As they walked in, a knock on the wardrobe door, then entered the nightmare...
'Once a dream, once a curse, once again I'll never leave!'

India Ellis-Trott (12)
Darton College, Barnsley

Charlie

I woke in the night to see my friends playing a game. 'What game is it?' I asked with sleep in my eye.

'Charlie,' they replied.

So I went over and asked, 'Charlie, are you there?'

Suddenly, the window slammed open and a ghost came in, it looked at the board. We got up and ran to the door. When the door slammed in our faces we jumped for the window, then Joe got impaled by Charlie. 'No!' I shouted. I went for him when I saw India crying. I didn't attack him I just ran.

Charlie Hague (11) & Bonnie

Darton College, Barnsley

Scary Skate Park

There were five friends playing peacefully in the skatepark. There were bikes, scooters and skateboards going up and down the ramps. There were lots of white figures. They were ghosts. They got four of the friends. One left and ran as fast as he could, but the ghost ran after him. He got away. He found an abandoned shed. He went in, the ghost passed him by. He saw the light switch and he turned it on. He stopped there all night, but in the middle of the night the ghost killed him.

'Get up!' Mum said.

Callum Cook (11)

Darton College, Barnsley

Don't Hold Your Breath

My head shook vigorously in icy water, loosening the hand gripped at my nape, sharp nails digging into my flesh. The only source of life escaped from my lips, trying to scream for help. With aching lungs struggling for air, my lips tempted to part. A gulp of fresh air was all it craved. My heart thudded as though it would burst. Open in defeat, letting him win. As time went on, pitch-black darkness filled my vision, a ghastly figure nearing towards me; it was probably Death. It suddenly happened at once; my eyelids closing, inhaling my final breath.

Habibah Haque
Jaamiatul Imaam Muhammad Zakaria School, Bradford

Mental Abuse To Humans

I sauntered into the teacher's room, the tables were cluttered, exam papers were flying everywhere and the dim light didn't help one bit. I slumped onto the wooden chair, burying my face in my hands. I felt feeble, dizzy. With heavy drooping eyes, I glanced up. A stained, marked book was placed in front of me. Reluctantly, I opened to the page highlighted by a red, sticky note... there it was. The words made my stomach churn. *Q8: What's 9+10? 21. Teacher's comment: It's not that hard!* She was lying to me. I knew it. I broke down... and cried.

Naimah Nasir (13)
Jaamiatul Imaam Muhammad Zakaria School, Bradford

Bad Dream

One step I take, the floorboard creaks. I look up at my surroundings. A whistling sound can be heard. I look right, *bang!* The window opens wide. I hear a terrifying howl. All of a sudden I hear another sound, I look down and see a fat rat scurrying away. I'm confused, one minute ago I was on my sofa reading a book. And now? Suddenly, the floorboard cracks. 'Argh!' I am falling in mid-air. All that can be seen is war and chaos. Whilst screaming, I awaken, giving Mother a fright.

Sidrah Zubair (14)

Jaamiatul Imaam Muhammad Zakaria School, Bradford

Nightmare Alley

The mahogany-coloured door slowly creaked open. There stood a pale humanistic figure in the darkness. I crept up the irregular pathway to find out what was happening. As I approached the door my nerves started to get the better of me. I could feel myself being hauled inside. It was like something had taken control over me. I cautiously entered the ancient house. Step after step my anxiety grew. I could see someone holding something. A stick, a knife? Was this woman a murderer? I could hear my heart pumping quickly. Myself breathing! Suddenly, I woke up!

Neelam Bachani (13)

Jaamiatul Imaam Muhammad Zakaria School, Bradford

1, 2, 3... You're Dead!

I lay in bed staring with fright. The wind howled. The leaves shuffled about. What a peculiar sight. The moon. It was a full moon tonight. Wolves howled in the creepy forest. The dark black clouds speedily crossed the moon. It was silent. Until… missiles fired, women and kids screamed. It was midnight. What do I do? I ran out of my house. Screamed for help. No reply. The shooting was coming nearer every second. It stopped. It was silent. Nothing, not even the trees swayed. Everything petrified. I turned around. 'You're next!' bellowed a voice from behind! *Blast!*

Amani Rashid

Jaamiatul Imaam Muhammad Zakaria School, Bradford

Have I Got A Last Chance?

I am bored! So I set off towards my friend's house. As I opened the door, my black cat stared at me cautiously with his cautious eyes! Whilst I was walking, disturbing sounds began to echo as I was passing by a strange place covered in darkness with a humongous, haunting gate. Somehow, my body was negative to enter, however I ignored this feeling and did what I desired. As the gate creaked open, the light of the moon reflected on a black figure stood silently staring at me with his eerie eyes. Was it my last breath or not?

Aisha Jabeen Bahar (13)

Jaamiatul Imaam Muhammad Zakaria School, Bradford

Deep In The Castle's Secret

Creak went the door... As I stepped into the gloomy castle, I heard echoes of the wind entering through the cracks of the wall. I continued to amble through the murky corridors until I heard a loud bang above. I steadily walked up the steep steps and came across a series of doors. Ahead I could see a luminous light under the crack. I approached it hesitantly. There was an eerie squeak from the door as a tall dark figure laughed sinisterly. There was a loud explosion. Then a familiar voice exclaimed, 'Hello sweetheart!' It was my outgoing, bonkers dad!

Thaniah Tasneem (13)
Jaamiatul Imaam Muhammad Zakaria School, Bradford

Death Approach

It was a monday morning as I was abandoned in a steel cage in an overcast room flushed with knives and chairs. I tried to bolt but realised I had no legs. Suddenly, the creaky door disclosed vastly and footsteps were approaching from the distance. My heart beat like a drum. I was frightened. The light flickered on and off as the moderate boy in the striped pyjamas grasped his hands towards me. I was raised higher and higher until I was above the bin. He peeled my orange skin and flung it into the bin.

Aaminah Patel (12)
Jaamiatul Imaam Muhammad Zakaria School, Bradford

Fight For Your Life

Slowly, the white clad figure began to proceed towards me, its every step bringing my dreadful fate closer. Suddenly, it stopped dead in its tracks, sniffing the air like a savage animal. My heart began to beat as fast as an out of control washing machine, maybe faster. I thought I had a chance and began to run, stumbling over tree roots. Finally reaching an old oak tree, I began to climb it. As I was sitting, hardly daring to breathe, I heard a rustling sound below. I jumped down and realised I was facing a stone brick wall. Trapped!

Amatullah Bint-Nisar (12)
Jaamiatul Imaam Muhammad Zakaria School, Bradford

Breakfast Time!

As she poured a white ghost-like liquid on top of me, I began to soften and soften, my sweetness went from me. Slowly, she picked me up in a cold, silver, metal object. From light suddenly it turned dark, after a few seconds two giant white boulders crushed me and crunched me down into little pieces. I was still alive, but couldn't see, just feel. Soon I felt myself sliding down a very unusual slimy slide, it was like a jelly jungle junction. *Crash!* I was in the pit of doom. After a few seconds I heard her say, 'Mmmmm!'

Almaas Randeri (12)
Jaamiatul Imaam Muhammad Zakaria School, Bradford

On The Run...

It was dark and I didn't know what I was running towards. The ear-splitting roar behind me grew louder and felt closer. I stumbled and the cold, hard ground pinched my face. It was stomping towards me. I needed to move. I reluctantly fled for dear life. A weak light uncovered the walls and floor. There was one reason for it. A way out. But I could see its shadow now, lumbering towards me, ready. Please, just a little longer. I could hear the waves and see the inky black sky. I was nearly there. But I never made it.

Kulthoom Ravat (13)

Jaamiatul Imaam Muhammad Zakaria School, Bradford

Just Like Any Ordinary...

A figure lurked out. Then I was snatched away. I heard the rattle of coins. Then I was gone. I suffered endless pain. First, a few bites on my face. Then I was bashed around everywhere viciously like I was practically not alive. My head was now ripped open, blood oozed out, flesh crumbled down into bits. My lips began to swell as teacups and iron were jammed against my mouth. The skin from my back began to peel, I was forced to lie down on layers of rigid rocks. After all, I was just an ordinary doll in a playhouse.

Mazeda Khanom (13)

Jaamiatul Imaam Muhammad Zakaria School, Bradford

The Unexpected Surprise!

One stormy night a boy was watching TV. Suddenly, there was a *bang!* on the door. The boy got up and checked through the window if anyone was there, but no one was. He was petrified. He went really slowly until he reached the door handle. He breathed in and breathed out. He opened it slowly. Guess who it was, he was shocked and surprised. It was SpongeBob. He let SpongeBob in and he had tea with him. Then SpongeBob started giggling and said, 'Bye.'
The boy said, 'Where do you live?'
'I'm your new neighbour.'
'OK, bye!'

Nazifa Akther Noor (12)
Jaamiatul Imaam Muhammad Zakaria School, Bradford

Eyes Closed!

Dorothy never spoke, a mute child she was called. Mrshone, Elizabeth and her, our new housekeepers cooked, cleaned, farmed our isolated, cold mansion home because Mother was alone, terrified and ill. Tommy and I played and prayed amongst the dark nights by candlelight. We found dusty documents and prehistoric photographs, people who had died would get their photo taken all dressed up but eyes closed. We hated those. Soon Mother went mental, sorrowful and sick. Mrshone, Ellie and Dorothy came to play, still mouth sewn shut. She found photos dated 1702, a picture of herself but with eyes closed!

Ishrat Siddiqah
Jaamiatul Imaam Muhammad Zakaria School, Bradford

Life Threat...

My heart hammered against my chest. I couldn't see where it had gone. Leaning against the rock sheltering me, I took a deep breath. I looked up and spotted two bright yellow eyes. I only looked into them for a second but they burnt through me like a laser. I rested my long tail behind me. The moon shone down on me, failing to make things any brighter. An ear-piercing scream ripped through the night. This was it. I waited; waited for the claws I had dreaded my entire life, to glide down, scoop me up and fly away.

Hamnah Nadeem (14)

Jaamiatul Imaam Muhammad Zakaria School, Bradford

The Doll

Did you hear that? It's the thing that my parents gave me as a 'present'. It has dancing eyes, chapped lips and weary, red circles on the balls of its cheeks. I said it was 'good', but now it's just plain evil. It had evil written all over it. It wakes up in the night. You can hear its childish laugh and its eerie rhymes. It scares me. I throw it out of my room, down the stairs, run back to my room and lock the door. Silence, then locks click, handles turn, the door creaks with a childish laugh...

Aleeza Nawab-Bibi Sabir Amin

Jaamiatul Imaam Muhammad Zakaria School, Bradford

Helpless!

'Argh!' I scream, whilst falling down a damp, narrow, sunless hole. *Thump!* 'Ouch, that hurt.' As I gradually stand up, I survey the room. The thick cobwebs above me, shattered glass around me, an unbearable reek in the air. Over in the corner, a book is laid on the desk. Surprisingly no dust on it. As I reach my arms to hold it I get a shiver of someone's presence. I turn around panting to see a dragging, murky figure. No face. No arms. Just a shadowy, starless cloak, floating rapidly towards me. I fall to the ground helplessly. 'Heeelllpp!'

Sumaiya Thamanna Khatun (14)
Jaamiatul Imaam Muhammad Zakaria School, Bradford

Ice Floor

I can feel my feet dragging on the cold, icy floor! Screams are let out from all directions. I've never tried this, I regret trying it too. I can hear sharp sounds, like a thorn being scraped along a piece of silk. My heart thumping, knowing I could slip and fall anytime soon, I keep hold of something sticky and cold. Immediately I remove my hands and *bang!* My head hits the freezing floor and silence! I can feel a large number of eyes staring straight at me! I did try to keep my balance. I seriously need ice skating lessons!

Fizzah Hasan-Daya
Jaamiatul Imaam Muhammad Zakaria School, Bradford

Trouble Attacks!

As I'm picking up speed, my engine gets louder and louder... My eyes brighten as I go higher and higher! Suddenly, I stop. Oh no! I'm in for it now! It's too late and within a flash I'm gone! All the screaming and shouting is getting to me! I can't control myself! Darkness has now come up us all and I can feel the tension building up inside me! Minutes later I feel a little more relaxed and my body loosens up. The pain is now entering in for a second time! I can't take it anymore! Why me?

Aishah Mahmood

Jaamiatul Imaam Muhammad Zakaria School, Bradford

Kipper

It sounded like water was trickling. Was it coming from the bathroom or the kitchen sink? It was getting louder second by second. It can't have been from the kitchen sink as I was lying in bed upstairs. The road was quiet which made me feel even more scared. What was I thinking? I just wouldn't fall asleep. It sounded as if it was from my room, in my room under my bed. I started to scream for 'Kipper' but he didn't come. Why? Why not today? He normally came when I needed him. I looked. He was dripping, *dead!*

Aaminah Abdul Maajid Rawat (13)

Jaamiatul Imaam Muhammad Zakaria School, Bradford

The Graveyard Ghost

I was walking across the creepy graveyard. There was a shiver going up my spine. I could hear footsteps of the dead. *Stomp. Stomp. Stomp.* I heard a scream. I could see a bright light in the distance. A cool breeze of wind swept across my face. I shivered. I thought it was Andy trying to play a joke on me, but everything seemed too scary for joke. 'Andy?' I whispered. 'Andy?' There was no reply. I felt a tap on my shoulder. I jumped! I wondered who it was. I turned around slowly...

Humaira Sagir (12)

Jaamiatul Imaam Muhammad Zakaria School, Bradford

Dead End...

I didn't know why they were after me. I didn't know what I did. My heart was beating as fast as a cheetah. Snow began to fall; within seconds a soft, cold, cushioned blanket lay on the ground. I turned back. They weren't there anymore. I ran in relief, however I caught a dark silhouette coming my way. It was one of them. I turned back in my previous direction and made a run for it. I stopped suddenly. A tall, brown wall stood in front of me and I realised I was surrounded. Now was my time to die...

Aqsa Rafique (12)

Jaamiatul Imaam Muhammad Zakaria School, Bradford

Keep An Eye Out!

The thunder was getting closer. I was at the right place, where I was told to come. It looked abandoned. It hadn't been touched ever! Phil told me to come here. I was praying that I wasn't alone at midnight. The weather was deteriorating. There was a building in sight, so I thought of taking shelter. As I entered, a spider's web attacked my face. Walking extremely slowly I carried on, creaking floorboards everywhere. Apprehensively, I turned around. Nope, still nothing. Something skimmed past me. It said, 'Beware!' I turned once more to see an unusual, peculiar, black figure. *Gulp!*

Shamima Uddin (14)
Jaamiatul Imaam Muhammad Zakaria School, Bradford

Those Horrible Green Things!

As they smelt smoke, they looked at each other with a shiver and ran down. *Bang! Bang! Slam!* It was all set out and ready. When they ran in they were shocked. At first it was a good feeling, but the horror on their faces told the whole story. They were almost out of breath, as fear ran over them, they started getting sweaty. The green slimy things just watched, the atmosphere was hot, they looked everywhere for an exit. As they wanted to make their escape, a voice called out, 'Sit down right now and eat all your veggies!'

Majida Rahman (13)
Jaamiatul Imaam Muhammad Zakaria School, Bradford

The Birthday Cake

I was sitting on a table so calmly until I saw a gigantic knife slicing into me. The candles blew out. The blood burst out and it was dripping hurriedly onto a plate. I was sitting on a reflective surface. In the background all I could hear were people singing. There was a five-year-old boy sitting in front of me with a fork in his hands. I started to panic. He dabbed the fork into my cream, fluffy top. The last thing I saw was a big, dark, gloomy cave with little white shining rocks inside it.

Syeda Ameena Khatun (12)

Jaamiatul Imaam Muhammad Zakaria School, Bradford

The Search For 'It'

'No!' Laura screamed as she pushed past the crowd, sweat dripping down her scarlet cheeks. 'It's gone!'
'But it's locked safely away, nobody knows except me,' I said.
Panicking she exclaimed, 'Must... find!'
It wasn't found, however she'd been gone for countless days. With swollen feet and aching arms, she still had the courage to search. Three years later... She blinked once, then twice. There it was, a few metres away from her. *Bang!* Within the blink of an eye, Laura was on the ground with a puddle of red blood around her. Someone killed her...
'Me! I stole it.'

Sophia Amira Hussain (12)

Jaamiatul Imaam Muhammad Zakaria School, Bradford

Hide And Scream

Amanda saw a demon inside the train, but suddenly it vanished. 'Weird,' she muttered, but nothing was getting in the way of Amanda and her friends having fun in Manchester. Thunder clapped as Amanda fell asleep. She had a dream about the demon. 'Kill the girl,' boomed a voice, 'otherwise you're dead as well!' The demon gave a shriek of fear and ran off. Amanda looked up and saw the demon in her face. She screamed and fainted. She woke up and was being dragged by chains. Choking, she realised she was being dragged to a pile of her friends' bodies...

Ridhwana Chowdhury (11)
Jaamiatul Imaam Muhammad Zakaria School, Bradford

The Last Surprise For Me...

Running through the isolated weather I reached home. I flung the keys out of my coat pocket and put it through the keyhole. As I gave the key a gentle twist, the door wouldn't unlock. After trying for a couple of minutes I began to lose hope, my fingers began to blister. I felt a cold breeze of wind brush past my ear. Then I heard footsteps coming closer. I turned around and there I saw my auntie with a razor-sharp knife... My heart pounded as tension stabbed through me. I closed my eyes and that was the end...

Ridwanah Sabi-Miah (11)
Jaamiatul Imaam Muhammad Zakaria School, Bradford

Death Is To Come!

As I got launched onto the kitchen table, I saw a mysterious figure open a cabinet from beneath me. It pulled out a sharp weapon. As the atmosphere around me got humid, I felt sweat dripping down me. The figure came closer and closer and I was sliced into six pieces. I then felt a sudden breeze, as the hot breath touched me. I felt so squished as I was grabbed with huge, filthy hands. Within a few seconds I was gone, chewed up forever. As I went from this wonderful world, I was remembered as the pink icing cake.

Fatema Sumaiya (12)
Jaamiatul Imaam Muhammad Zakaria School, Bradford

The Disappearing Figure

It was dark and gloomy and the street was quiet. The wind gushed through the trees heavily, making a creepy noise as suddenly lightning struck. Lily and Layla were all alone in the mansion, with no one there. They lived happily and knew what to do when they got scared, but that night something strange happened. There was a flash! A figure appeared; it looked extremely terrifying. It was wearing all black. Two seconds later it vanished. The girls were petrified. The next second it was behind them. Slowly lifting his hand, the figure brought the knife down...

Maimuna Ali (11)
Jaamiatul Imaam Muhammad Zakaria School, Bradford

Beast

Its grimy ears were as razor-sharp as a knife. Its greasy green hair was filled with slimy yellow earwax. Dribbling out of its hideous nose were gooey, gruesome bogeys. Its evil eyes were as vivid red as blood. Its oversized mouth was half there and half ripped off leaving behind a sinister smile. Its pruny fingers were covered with its mortifying nails as black as coal. It was a devilish, monstrous beast. I bolted as fast as lightning, hoping terribly that I could find my way out of its sight. However, unfortunately for me it was too late.

Afia Ahmed (12)

Jaamiatul Imaam Muhammad Zakaria School, Bradford

The Hook

'Awoo...' The moon was full and Lilly was out alone. On a sinister hill, there stood a house. Through the window a radiant light shone. Lilly realised something. A shadow stood glaring at Lilly. *Boom!* Lightning struck the house and the shadow vanished. In the corner of her eyes she found a smashed window. Carefully she climbed through the jagged window. A dim light flickered on in one of the rooms. Lilly walked towards it. Goosebumps covered her body and a drop of sweat rolled down her cheek. Hook grabbed her. The night ended with deafening screams!

Nusrat Kamali (12)

Jaamiatul Imaam Muhammad Zakaria School, Bradford

Tonsil Terror

Bang! The thunder clashed loudly. Emily was asleep. The lightning made her wake up and she couldn't asleep. 'Great,' she muttered, 'now I'll never go back to sleep.' She lay in bed but she noticed that her room looked... different. It smelt, it felt moist. She tried to realise what was different but something grabbed her and dragged her down. It pushed her down a spongy slide. She screamed. She saw two bells hanging down. She tried to grab one but lost her grip. She realised where she was when she landed with a loud splash in a pool...

Nimaa Mussa (11)

Jaamiatul Imaam Muhammad Zakaria School, Bradford

The Long Way Home

Hannah ran, ran and kept on running. She didn't know where she was going. She could feel the devilish demon's breath hit her. Was she running towards more danger? She felt helpless. Cautiously, she turned around to see what was behind her and caught a black, ugly beast chasing after her. She was trapped in danger. She tried running faster and faster but she couldn't. The beast was as ugly as something she could never imagine. Her heart was as fast as lightning. A shiver ran down her spine. Then she ended up doing something she could never imagine doing.

Humayra Begum (11)

Jaamiatul Imaam Muhammad Zakaria School, Bradford

Lost...

Rose turned around, gasped in horror and then ran, edging closer and closer to the forbidden grounds. What had got into her? Suddenly, a so-called Death Hound circled her, sniffing. Its hideous eyes were locked on Rose and strings of saliva trailed from its dagger-like teeth. Without hesitation, she crossed the forbidden line – there was no going back now. Out of nowhere, a cold hand touched her shoulder, passing a waning chill down her spine. Rose quivered, 'He-lp,' she cried. But, before she could talk again, her voice broke and she was in a pool of her own blood...

Saarah Bhana (12)
Jaamiatul Imaam Muhammad Zakaria School, Bradford

The Life Of Horror

I was running and running as fast as I could. But it kept getting closer and closer to me. Suddenly, I came towards a spine-chilling well. I had no choice but to sacrifice my precious life. Within a blink of an eye I was falling and falling through the narrow hole of filthy water. A mouth was wide open below me. I had reached my destination: a deep, dark belly. I realised I wasn't the only one in here. I saw two bright red eyes watching me suffer my pains. This was the very end of my life.

Hajra Patel (11)
Jaamiatul Imaam Muhammad Zakaria School, Bradford

The Night To Remember

Psychopathic giggles of creepy girls in spine-chilling masks ran around the forest and their leader had a cloth over him and an axe. *Bang!* A loud shooting noise was made. 'One down, nineteen to go.' Running fast like a cheetah through the eerie trees, trying to silence her breath, gasping with fear but still concentrating on them. She ran faster as she saw them coming closer. She fell on the muddy floor, dragged her body and cleaned herself. When she started to sprint an axe charged at her. Blood flew everywhere... You can still hear a faint deadly screech.

Radyah Choudhury (12)
Jaamiatul Imaam Muhammad Zakaria School, Bradford

Bone-Scraper

There was a legend once told of a bone-scraper that lived in a cave near my house one million years ago. People started to go inside the cave to discover the history of cavemen. Some people said the spirit of the bone-scraper still haunts it. My parents kept telling me, 'Don't go near the cave!' But one day I got sick of listening to them, I wanted to explore the cave so I went in. I had this petrifying feeling something was there, watching me every step of the way. Then, suddenly, a fleshless hand grabbed me...

Hazmah Hajee (11)
Jaamiatul Imaam Muhammad Zakaria School, Bradford

Tension

'Argh!' The scream pierced through my ears. My heart popped like a needle popping a balloon. As I walked towards the tattered door I heard the droplets of rain seeping through the ceiling. I wasn't alone, and my friend was somewhere within the abandoned warehouse. 'Argh!' There went the scream again, this time sweat trickled down my forehead as I walked towards the old, brown door. The floorboards creaked as I twisted the doorknob. I could see a shadow swiftly slither across as I peeked through the keyhole. With great courage I opened the door and 'Argh...!'

Jannatun Nisa

Jaamiatul Imaam Muhammad Zakaria School, Bradford

The Doom Of Darkness

As he picked me up I got quite frightened, he then gave me a big boost. I went flying across the other side and got quite bruised. I stopped. I glared around to see what was around me. It was pitch-black so I couldn't see anything. I thought I could see red blazing eyes just staring at me. Also I could hear the rustling sound of the crispy leaves coming closer and closer towards me. He then picked me back up with his gentle hands and I was so relieved. What am I?

Aisha Khalifa (12)

Jaamiatul Imaam Muhammad Zakaria School, Bradford

Life In A Deadly Place

A piercing shriek clung to the air... I spun around just in time to notice a pair of razor-sharp fangs set feast into a large pile of fresh meat! Suddenly, the creature turned, realising my presence... blood was splattered all over its face, green, oozing pus squirted from its eyes. Chunks of meat fell from its claws as it took a few steps towards me! I stood paralysed, fear stabbed my heart... I knew just then that my life was over... 'Ken, where are you?' I screamed for help.
The creature came closer, growling, 'I'm right here, Barbie!'
'Argh!'

Tahira Khan
Jaamiatul Imaam Muhammad Zakaria School, Bradford

Stuck! Save Me

I'm lost in darkness, I can't see anything. I'm crouching down onto my knees, I've got a cramp. I need air, I can't breathe. Suddenly, I hear children talking and footsteps coming closer. I hear a strange sound clicking continuously. I feel I can move myself slightly, just a few clicks. I see light, I'm beaming with happiness! I can feel the freedom running towards me. I'm getting lifted up like I'm in an elevator and my legs slowly straighten, I can have a long stretch. The first words that come out from my sound box, 'Pop goes the weasel.'

Abida Siddiqua (13)
Jaamiatul Imaam Muhammad Zakaria School, Bradford

One Night

One gloomy night Lilly couldn't fall asleep. She tossed and turned but then gave up, so she decided to go downstairs for a sip of water. Scared to death, she bravely tiptoed down the stairs. Whilst walking down she tripped over something, then saw the object glow. It was only her cat. Lilly had regretted going downstairs. She thought of going back up but decided not to. When she reached the kitchen, she struggled finding the switch, but finally found it. Slowly, she turned the dim light on, but hadn't seen what she expected and shockingly someone screamed...

Malakah Al-Korj (11)
Jaamiatul Imaam Muhammad Zakaria School, Bradford

The Follower That Lived In The Forest

It was Sunday, the sun was shining and the water looked inviting. I made my way to the forest, thinking it was a great idea. I started walking, seeing the beautiful nature around me. Soon, I recognised that a shadow was following me. *Probably just my imagination,* I thought, so I carried on walking. This time the shadow tapped me! I let out a loud shriek and looked behind me to see a man. A man the colour of danger, ready to conclude my life. I ran faster, looking for a shortcut around the forest, but it was too late...

Tasneem Begum (12)
Jaamiatul Imaam Muhammad Zakaria School, Bradford

Cliffhanger...

She ran, just ran, and kept on running. She knew *it* was getting closer and closer, and realised it would eventually grab her anyway. But at this point her only chance was to run. She could feel her navy jeans beginning to stick to her legs from the tormenting sun which was blazing down. Just the thought of it made her gag and nearly throw up. But, suddenly, she came to the edge of the cliff. 1000 feet away from the ground, her heart began to thump. She stepped forward to jump, but it was too late...

Aleema Ali (11)
Jaamiatul Imaam Muhammad Zakaria School, Bradford

The Mysterious Shadow!

The dark fearful shadow was moving closer and closer as I ran as fast as a tiger! Not glimpsing back I thought to myself, *Who could it be? A wolf? Or a fox?* Not knowing who, I started to run faster. I could hear long, deep breaths chase me. I could hear the trees rustle and bustle as the strong wind blew. A few leaves covered my face, which made me fall over a twig. I laid on the ground, not knowing what to do. The shadow vanished. When getting up, I walked and realised it was my own shadow!

Aisha Khan (13)
Jaamiatul Imaam Muhammad Zakaria School, Bradford

Unknown

The wind was howling, the fog was chasing and I was running. I was running as fast as I could to get away from it, but still it came closer and closer. I ran past the church, through the forest and realised that I was going in circles. I stopped running for a while and noticed that it wasn't there anymore. I was so scared. The fog became thicker and thicker and the wind became louder and stronger. I noticed a black shadow behind me which grew bigger and bigger. I felt a cold hand touching me. 'James, remember me?'

Haaniyah Zaheer (13)
Jaamiatul Imaam Muhammad Zakaria School, Bradford

What Am I...?

I was made and got put into a black coffin which had fiery, blazing fire. It burnt the base of my cylinder body. At last I was out of the suffocation, but then a big splat of red blood fell on me! Seconds later, needles were jabbed in my body. When I had time to breathe, I got put into a box of darkness and ended up in a gloomy house. I heard intimidating children who grabbed me and placed me on the grimy counter. A giant lit the needles, someone blew them out. *Munch!* I was in someone's stomach...

Aabedah Khatun (12)
Jaamiatul Imaam Muhammad Zakaria School, Bradford

Life After Death...

My helpless body was thrashed from side to side as the battered car tumbled down the hill. The windows smashed and the shattered glass sliced through my bruised flesh. The heat was so intense that it singed off the end of my hair. The red-hot flames licked at my skin, almost teasing. I opened my scorched mouth and an ear-splitting cry of agony escaped.

Another vulnerable soul coursed through mine, jolting me from my memories. Those haunted memories of my demise, that will never leave me. Not once, in my eternal death on the fields of sorrows.

Anisah Khanam (12)
Jaamiatul Imaam Muhammad Zakaria School, Bradford

The Haunted Mansion

I walked across the old, smelly road and entered a gigantic mansion. It was dark and spooky, webs everywhere and darkness spread above me. The door creaked open. I felt a shiver up my spine. I called out Lucy's name but no one answered. It was freezing cold. The floorboards creaked. I saw blood oozing down the wall. I looked up. There was Lucy hanging from the wall with her head cracked open. I was terrified. I felt pain and heard someone screaming from inside the room. I walked in and something grabbed my leg from under the carpet.

Iman Hussain (12)
Jaamiatul Imaam Muhammad Zakaria School, Bradford

Owl...

A shadow left Sienna surprised as she had never seen such a figure. Sienna took a step forward, still holding on what was in her sweaty, pale hand tightly. She wanted to continue forward but suddenly a hand stretched forward from the dull tree. Sienna gasped and struggled to free herself from this foreign creature. Sienna saw a bony, wrinkly corpse with sharp, brown nails. The clutched hand began to open like a rotting flower and had writing on it which Sienna could not read. She went a bit closer to read what it said: 'Can you be my friend?'

Tamanna Khanam (13)
Jaamiatul Imaam Muhammad Zakaria School, Bradford

The World Of Unknown

I should've taken the bus but I felt in the mood for an adventure so I took the path leading through the forest. While I was walking, I could hear the snapping of branches but when I looked back there was no one there. My heart beat louder and louder as I walked on trying to ignore it. Up ahead I could see a house. I decided to check it out. As I reached the door, it slowly creaked open so I stepped inside. *Bang!* The door slammed shut behind me. Oh no, I was trapped! What should I do?

Habibah Siddiqa Nawaz (14)
Jaamiatul Imaam Muhammad Zakaria School, Bradford

I Never Knew It Could Be Him!

A creepy noise echoed in my ear. I speedily forced myself out of my snuggly bed and slipped on the bed slippers. I could feel somebody walking towards me up the stairs. I kicked my slippers off and sprung into bed, making sure all of the sides of my duvet were tucked inwards. After a couple of seconds, I could feel the pin-drop silence so I peeked out by slightly lifting the corner of my duvet. I could vividly see a peculiar and spontaneous shadow. The lights flickered on. Standing there, was my little mischievous brother, sucking on a lollipop!

Wafa Mahar (14)
Jaamiatul Imaam Muhammad Zakaria School, Bradford

The Big Run

My body was sweating. I was drenched. They were running after me. Everything was blurred because of my speed. This body of mine didn't care about the pain ahead, it just kept running. Worry suffocated my face as it was catching up with me. I looked to my right, it was next to me. I looked to my left, there was another one. I couldn't escape. The only option was to keep running. The red gate came into sight. A breath of relief escaped as I ran past it. The crowd went wild – I had won!

Siddeeqah Tasneem (11)
Jaamiatul Imaam Muhammad Zakaria School, Bradford

That Night Away From Home

I sat there unpacking, figuring out what'll happen to her. Her scream pierced my ears. I wonder what'll be waiting for me. *Tick-tock! Chime!* The clock struck twelve as I made my way to the hall. Nobody there. I called out for Tom, no one was there. I was alone. As lightning struck the mansion, I felt a drop on my head. Then another. Then it all came gushing down. It was blood! *Bang!* The door slammed. I drowned in a pool of blood. Lightning struck three times. It was a sign, but it came too late. He reached me.

Maryam Shahid (12)

Jaamiatul Imaam Muhammad Zakaria School, Bradford

The Shadow

I'd been walking for a while but finally reached the centre of the woods. Lightning flashed and rain poured. A wolf howled in the distance. I saw a mysterious shadow lurking in the trees. I delved further in to investigate. I felt a prickly sensation on my back as if there was someone there. I looked behind, nothing. After some time I lit a fire and sat deep in thought. Suddenly, the fire went out. I was too petrified to move. Something pulled me. It dragged me into the forbidden part of the forest. I screamed for help. There was no hope.

Rameen Afzal (12)

Jaamiatul Imaam Muhammad Zakaria School, Bradford

The Cemetery Shortcut

I strode purposefully through the dead of night. Fog stole in from all sides. I had one ambition. Warily, I eyed the cemetery, frowning out of the gloom. Trembling, like a cornered vixen, I darted through the graves; seemingly laughing at my unease. All of a sudden, I glimpsed home. Light-headed with relief, I stumbled on. Without warning, my foot sunk into the crumbling earth. Staring down in horror, I saw a gaunt-faced skeleton leering up at me. The remains of a once live person. It hissed in a grating voice, 'Hello Lara, come and join me...' I shrieked terror-stricken.

Jasmine Hussain (12)
Jaamiatul Imaam Muhammad Zakaria School, Bradford

Baked By Fire

I screamed in agony as giant hands shoved me into a pit of fire. Why would anyone do this to me? Slowly, my creamy, soft flesh turned golden. My body started to go stiff and hard. *Ding!* After hours of pain and agony, the giant hands returned and freed me from the fire. *Splat!* A sugary, icing-like mixture was spread over my skin, cooling me down in just seconds. After that, a splash of colours decorated my skin like beads...
'Wow, these are amazing Mum, thanks,' exclaimed Jade, as she dug into the freshly baked batch of golden cupcakes.

Sumayyah Begum (11)
Jaamiatul Imaam Muhammad Zakaria School, Bradford

Last Sights...

It was the night before it all started. We were sitting together happily when the lights blackened! Eventually, it shone back on. Now that day has gone. Today, Friday 13th was the day it had all started. The lights flickered off! Images of death sprawled around me. My parents suddenly became quiet... I noticed droplets of fresh blood. I didn't click on! Argh! Then, it came for me! I was lost in the dark, no support, nothing... It hurled spears in every direction. I thought I was dead, but then the lights glimmered back on. My parents stood there... Frozen!

Faatimah Khan (12)
Jaamiatul Imaam Muhammad Zakaria School, Bradford

The Alley Of Doom

Lightning flashed as I trembled down the eerie alleys. It felt as if somebody was walking behind me and touching my back but every time I would turn back there would be nothing there. The wind bowled as the lightning flashed. I tripped on something hard and mysterious. It felt as if someone had put their foot there and tripped me up but there was nothing there. I started walking further down the alley until I came across a cottage. I carefully opened it with a loud, ear-bashing creak. There stood a white figure with blood everywhere. I'm dead now!

Afira Khan (11)
Jaamiatul Imaam Muhammad Zakaria School, Bradford

Black Baby

As I walked through the dark and rusted house, I saw a black doll sitting on a dusty table staring at me. I tried to run but the door slammed shut. I thought, *A doll can't do anything*, so I went past and realised that it turned its head to my direction. I screamed and it cackled. I turned my head 90 degrees and rapidly turned back. It wasn't there. I looked everywhere around me. When I looked up, it jumped off the cracked ceiling and onto my face, scratching and ruining it, leaving many scars.

Saalihah Ahmed Ravat (11)

Jaamiatul Imaam Muhammad Zakaria School, Bradford

The Fearful Multicoloured Door

When the exciting day came for the trip to the museum, we all got ready to go. As we drove I saw a colourful, creative door in the museum which made my brain and head feel funny. When I entered the multicoloured, picturesque door, I found a world full of zombies and an enormous ant which was coming closer and closer. I felt so terrified she picked me up ready to eat me but silly me, she put me near to her mouth so I could hear her. She said, 'Will you be my pet?' I nodded quietly...

Navira Imran (11)

Jaamiatul Imaam Muhammad Zakaria School, Bradford

Friday 13th

On Friday 13th the wind was howling like ghosts, as Sarah fell asleep gazing at the most horrifying ghostly movie. All of a sudden there was a knock on the door. Shaking with horror, like a tornado, she looked out of the window and saw a dark cloaked, ghostly figure. After witnessing that terrifying sight, Sarah went to the deserted street which was covered with fresh blood around her car. As she peeked through the shattered glass window of her car, she was in shock... Through her watery eyes she saw her beloved parent dead. Argh!

Yusraa Kayat (11)
Jaamiatul Imaam Muhammad Zakaria School, Bradford

Halloween Night

It was Halloween night and I was on my way to my next-door neighbour's house for trick or treat. *Knock. Knock.* 'I can't wait until they arrive at the door.' I knocked again but this time I was in for a big surprise. 'Argh!' I jumped up and ran towards the gate. Then, after a few minutes of panic, I shouted, 'Are you okay?' The door opened slowly, my heart was beating rapidly. Then, I saw the family watching a horror movie in the background. And that was my very embarrassing, funny Halloween.

Hafsa Siddiquie
Jaamiatul Imaam Muhammad Zakaria School, Bradford

The Mysterious Journey

I ran and ran as far as I could into the woods without noticing it.
I thought I was being followed but when I turned around, nothing
was there. I craved to go back to bed but it was too late. All I could
hear was blood-curdling howls, shrieks and screams so I stopped
and thought about it. Was I being tricked or was this real? 'Argh! I'm
gonna kill you!' a voice boomed. 'Mwahahahaaa!'
Was that the end of Chloe or is there more to discover? 'Make sure
you don't ever come knocking on my door, or else...'

Humaira Khanom (11)

Jaamiatul Imaam Muhammad Zakaria School, Bradford

The Girl With No Notice

One dark, scary night there was a 12-year-old schoolgirl named
Madison. She was strolling in a forest until she got to an abandoned
house. She looked through one of the windows and she saw a bright
light so she wanted to find out what it could be. As Madison opened
the door and walked inside, she heard a grizzly laugh which made
her shudder. She carried on walking along the corridor and stepped
inside the room with the light on. She bent down and saw it was a fire
and without a doubt she was gone... 'Argh!'

Hadia Zia (12)

Jaamiatul Imaam Muhammad Zakaria School, Bradford

Creak! What Was That?

Creak! The sound was getting closer. Each noise was a little louder than the one before. Suzie woke up with a start. What was it making that irritating sound. Her heart leapt into her throat. *Creak!* Silence. *Creak!* Silence. For now she had no doubt that someone or something was in the room coming nearer every second. *Creak!* Silence. *Creak!* Silence. Nearer and nearer. Suzie sat bolt upright and the moon had gone behind a cloud. Darkness had filled the room. She strained her eyes trying to see. Then she heard a voice. It whispered, 'Suzie, are you awake?'

Khadijah Patel (12)
Jaamiatul Imaam Muhammad Zakaria School, Bradford

The Shadows!

It was midnight, it was dark. The moon was out and I was walking in the spine-chilling forest, alone. I heard a mysterious whooshing sound and a cackle. I turned but there was nothing to be seen. I continued walking. This time a loud, long cackle was made, something tapped my back. I turned slowly and saw a dark figure with shining, yellow eyes. It smiled and chuckled, 'Wrong place.' It grabbed me, my eyes closed. All of a sudden my eyes opened, I was in a box. It was a coffin. I screamed! I was alone! Forever!

Sanaa Akhtar (11)
Jaamiatul Imaam Muhammad Zakaria School, Bradford

Demons Do Exist!

'Demons are fake!' I exclaimed.
'There are such things, come to the cemetery today at 5,' Ryan yelled.
'Beware!' was carved onto the sign. 'Ryan?' I yelled.
'Boo!' he shouted.
'Argh!' I screeched.
'I'm a demon,' Ryan said.
'Go away!' I replied.
'I'm just playing around, come on, let's go inside.' Slowly I walked
forward, grabbing onto Ryan like a mother grabbing onto its baby
bear. 'Don't worry, Kia,' Ryan said reassuringly. Then a hand was
placed on mine and Ryan's shoulder. We froze like ice statues.
'I've been waiting for your arrival!' a voice boomed. 'Say goodbye to
this world!'

Syeda Zainab Hussain (11)

Jaamiatul Imaam Muhammad Zakaria School, Bradford

Alone

Bang! There it is again. Why won't this creature leave me alone?
My parents aren't here. I am alone. What can I do? The creature
is chasing me around the house. I am out of breath. Suddenly, I
collapse. Long nails poking into my skin, making a river of blood
around me. I know I am going to die here all alone. I lose a lot of
blood. Slowly my eyes begin to close and I am dead. The creature
laughs and says, 'Who's going to move into this house next and be
my prey so I can kill them?'

Saara Ahmed (11)

Jaamiatul Imaam Muhammad Zakaria School, Bradford

Life Or Death

The fogginess from afar blurred my vision. Not knowing what to do, I waited silently for Ben to arrive. The silence ended when the church bell rang out of nowhere. Who could this possibly be? It was late night and no one was to be seen anywhere. *Clatter! Clapper!* I heard from behind. It grew louder. 'Ben!' I called out, then suddenly my voice froze. My legs started dragging me up the stairs of the church. I soon reached the top. Down beneath me lay an empty grave with a coffin waiting. Not knowing what possessed me, I fell down.

Anisa Anjum (12)
Jaamiatul Imaam Muhammad Zakaria School, Bradford

Trapped

My hair sat on my shoulders. It was dripping with sweat. Hands trembling, legs shaking, I could sense him. But how could I be so sure it was him? Ominously, I turned my head to the left, then to the right... All clear! I quickened my pace. Under the glittering glow of the moon, I noticed a shadow lying on the floor. It was edging closer towards me. I paused for a second. The shadow stopped. I stepped back. The shadow copied. I felt as if 1000 creatures were closing in on me. 'Hello?' *Bang! Thump!* I was trapped...

Adiba Kamali (12)
Jaamiatul Imaam Muhammad Zakaria School, Bradford

The Demon Child

'Mum, when are you going to give me my gift for my birthday?' Emily asked her mum.

'Be patient, you will get it soon,' exclaimed Emily's mum.

That night, her Mum came to her room and put a necklace around her.

The next morning she woke up and had a strange pain in her neck. Lifting herself was as hard as lifting rocks. When she opened her eyes, she saw a small black figure sitting in front of her smiling. She rubbed her eyes. It had vanished. She quickly got out of bed and a large black figure loomed over her...

Noor Tariq Sheikh (11)
Jaamiatul Imaam Muhammad Zakaria School, Bradford

Poisonous Plague

It spread around; red rashes, black blotches and led to deaths in three days. Its poison sinked deep into everyone's blood and slowly made it rot away. The plague was something everyone feared. Goodbye to the one who released it into the air, as it slowly multiplied and killed many prisoners with its rage. It spread around London, England and Europe. In hope of finding a body to engulf it. Hoping for new, earthy, sweet blood in its hungry system. Human body was what it craved for. Its army took over the world and filled it with the poisonous plague.

Anika Begum (12)
Jaamiatul Imaam Muhammad Zakaria School, Bradford

Mysterious Graveyard

It started with lightning... Come play with me! Come play with me! Come play with me!

Mary made a sharp turn. An executed, rotten head rolled beside her spilling blood in the haunted graveyard. Mist surrounded the area. Voices, murmurs, everything haunted her thoughtless brain. What was going on? She wasn't alone. The gate banged shut. Black bats dropped to the crisp, green grass next to terrified Mary. Their wings were cut off and eyes screwed out. No ears visible. Her soul was drifting away. The clock struck midnight. *Ding!* The bloody, black figure approached her from the frightening past...

Eman Fatima Azam

Jaamiatul Imaam Muhammad Zakaria School, Bradford

The Doll House

Jason ventured around the remote, snowy, crystal streets. He spotted a strange, bright doll shop as he stared into the shop's window. By surprise, twinkling music played as a doll twirled with features exactly like his. He bolted towards the door, he found it locked. He had the idea of aiming frosted snowballs at the door to open it. His plan miserably failed, but, by surprise a bell rang. A miracle occurred. The door opened, he crept in and grabbed the doll. Memories flew back to his mind. When his plastic eyeballs itched, he realised he had become a doll...

Rumeswa Rehman Shakeel (12)

Jaamiatul Imaam Muhammad Zakaria School, Bradford

The Evil Man

There was once a young boy and his two twin sisters. The boy died and his two sisters remained. They were adopted by a horrible, evil old man who made them work all day. Every day he forced them to clean top to bottom and they didn't get any food or money. They had to go to the haunted streets and find food to feed themselves. One evening, he left the house with terrifying laughter and never came back that day. Shocking noises came through the brick walls. The house was surrounded by bloodthirsty, old, nasty looking zombies!

Anisah Begum (11)
Jaamiatul Imaam Muhammad Zakaria School, Bradford

Who's There?

I decided to enter it, the dark, gloomy, mysterious forest. I could hear the leaves rustle as I walked upon them. Feeling the wind swift past my ears, I looked left and right but could not see anything through the misty fog. I continued my journey, however I felt a shiver going down my spine. I started to run when suddenly a black figure zoomed past me. My heart started to beat rapidly. Hearing the leaves rustle behind me, I yelled, 'Who's there?' but there was no reply. I turned around to go back home, however I never arrived...

Hafsa Shoaib (12)
Jaamiatul Imaam Muhammad Zakaria School, Bradford

The Incredibly Dark Shadow!

I saw a shadow from where I was standing. It was remotely far and every time I looked there it was coming closer. I could feel a chill running down my spine. Out of nowhere, it started to rain heavily. A flash of lightning struck the dark figure. I could hear a loud howling noise behind me. What was going to happen? Suddenly, it went dark. I couldn't see anything. My head was stuck in a rough fabric. I couldn't breathe. I was suffocating. I tried to get out but it was tied too tight. 'Oh no! Help!'

Safiyyah Rawat (12)
Jaamiatul Imaam Muhammad Zakaria School, Bradford

Begin!

The threatening teacher came closer towards me. Eyes filled with hatred plunged into my inner soul. As hands reached out like enormous trees, he placed something in front of me. One look at it had already paralysed me. My terrified body tried to start, however I knew I couldn't. A boiling heat wave swarmed across my face. The menacing teacher walked towards me and stood in front of me. Words raged out like a caged bird, words like no other shook the entire room. 'You may begin your exam!' he roared with a threatening voice. I knew I was dead!

Faiza Hussain (11)
Jaamiatul Imaam Muhammad Zakaria School, Bradford

Test Papers – The Scariest, Most Terrifying Creatures Of All...

The menacing teacher stood at the front of the classroom towering above us like a giant. A sheath of murderous, formal papers were clutched in her arms. 'You have forty-five minutes for this test,' she explained. As she handed the papers out, my heart started to beat louder than a stampede of fully grown elephants. Blood was rushing to my head. My life had officially ended. Suddenly, a crisp, white sheet of paper fluttered gracefully down in front of me. 'You may start,' her brisk voice commanded. I gulped, breathing shakily and turned the petrifying beast over with trembling hands...

Tayyibah Saleem (11)

Jaamiatul Imaam Muhammad Zakaria School, Bradford

Speechless

In a lofty building, in room 24, it was all dusky and silent until the door slammed open and the light switched on. An opaque figure appeared. In an instant, it rushed towards me. It had steaming fire on its face and it had black eyes in fury. Its brown wrinkled hands swayed as it ran and its hair rocked side to side allowing miniature hair balls to fly around. Its mouth coated with yellow teeth opened. A revolting aroma surrounded the air. I was cemented to the floor in shock without question. It said, 'Have you done your homework?'

Jubayda Yasmin-Muhit (11)

Jaamiatul Imaam Muhammad Zakaria School, Bradford

Down, Down, Down It Goes!

There I was in a gigantic white pool with a horrific hole in the centre. I couldn't figure out where I was. From my point of view, I saw that the hole was darker than a pitch-black night. Suddenly, I saw a huge hand reach for a silver lever and then pull. In moments, water started gushing out from all sides, swirling and twirling around and around in circles. Then I opened my eyes, I couldn't see a thing. I was drenched in water. I realised that I had been flushed down the toilet... Down, down, down!

Javairia Hussain (12)
Jaamiatul Imaam Muhammad Zakaria School, Bradford

Vanished

'Argh...' her screams echoed and made the trees shake in fear. After that night she was never seen again until one night when the moon was full and the wind roared in anger. Lilly was exploring an abandoned house and discovered a secret room. As she climbed down the stairs, a gasp of wind hit her face. Cobwebs hid in the corner of the room as Lilly wandered through the cellar. *Crash!* Something fell. Feeling around, a drop of sweat rolled down her cheek. A pale face glared at her and an icy hand shot out and squeezed her tightly...

Sumaiya Alam
Jaamiatul Imaam Muhammad Zakaria School, Bradford

Serial Killer

I was sitting down with my photo album looking at some recent pictures. Suddenly, I noticed a sinister similarity. Mr Daniels, the new man in town, was in every single one, staring. I gasped as I realised he was in the window opposite. With a girl. He started slapping and beating her. He threw her to the ground. The killer stopped, raised a dagger and chopped her into tiny pieces. As he started eating the pieces, I ran downstairs. 'Hello?' a grim voice said. Mr Daniels. His mouth dripping blood. Eyes red. Both hands gripped my neck, tighter, tighter...

Mishkat Siddiqah (11)

Jaamiatul Imaam Muhammad Zakaria School, Bradford

Cut!

Britney walked down the lane. The birds were chirping and music drifted in the countryside. Suddenly, everything went pitch-black. There was nothing but silence. Then a deafening growl shattered it. Beads of sweat ran down Britney's neck. A figure staggered towards her. Not knowing what to do, she ran. Minutes passed, then a small creature scuttled across the road. 'Argh!' the figure yelped.
'Cut!' cried a voice. Seconds later, gigantic black boards were lifted from the ground and everything became light again. 'Let's take a retake!'
'What? Where am I?'
'You're in the middle of a movie set.'

Nahida Akther Noor (11)

Jaamiatul Imaam Muhammad Zakaria School, Bradford

Mystery Night

I rapidly bolted out of my terrifying house. Sweat dripped down my forehead. As I ran outside, a corpse lay in front of me. Everywhere I looked people were chasing and haunting me with their horrific faces. Lights flickered on and off. In the sinister street was a blood-curdling figure. The face was pale white with pitch-black strands of hair. Rain splashed down, lightning spread like the Black Death. Everywhere I ran I met with a horrible sight so I returned back to my bedroom. My mother strolled inside and enquired, 'Did you have a nice, spooky Halloween?'

Khalisa Fariha (11)
Jaamiatul Imaam Muhammad Zakaria School, Bradford

The Murder Scene

I stumble down the staircase fearing that a murderer is behind with a knife in his hand due to the news report last night. Suddenly, my cup drops and cracks in two pieces. I shriek. All of a sudden I hear a cringing noise opposite my direction, two knives being sharpened together. I yell out for help but nobody is coming. *Why does this always happen to me? It's so unfair!* I think. I manage to walk down the stairs. It's so annoying now that my foot is broken, why always me?

Fatima Rafiq Bismillah (13)
Jaamiatul Imaam Muhammad Zakaria School, Bradford

The Frightening Feature

Suddenly, the huge door flew wide open. I didn't know where I should go. Who should I call? All these questions in my mind that I couldn't answer. I thought I should go in, so that's what I did. I went inside and suddenly the door shut and the bright light vanished. I could hear creepy noises and see frightening shadows. I started crying and calling for help but no one could hear me. I started walking and stopped that minute when I felt a tap on my back...

Atikah Rana (12)

Jaamiatul Imaam Muhammad Zakaria School, Bradford

Untitled

It all started on the night of Halloween. I had just about finished watching three horror movies. I got up from my seat and I was extremely tired. I just about made it to my bed that night. I fell asleep very quickly but kept on waking up in the middle of the night with these scary nightmares. Then I got up and these long, sharp, metal nails were tapping and stroking my neck, blood was all over my covers and a scar was on my neck with my head dripping with sweat. I looked behind wondering who it was...

Junnaht Ahmed

Jaamiatul Imaam Muhammad Zakaria School, Bradford

My Frightening Night

It was night-time and it was really windy. I woke up and shivered. 'Sally?' I called. No answer.

I looked out of the window and saw a terrifying man in black saying, 'Lily, Lily, come out. I have a sword to kill you with.' I looked out of the window and saw the same man killing two people. I heard the door opening and heard a blood-curdling scream. I could only hear him saying, 'Lily, Lily.' I got so frightened. Then the man said, 'Lily, Lily, I am here.' The door opened, the man came towards me...

Ruqayah Iqbal (11)
Jaamiatul Imaam Muhammad Zakaria School, Bradford

The Mysterious Hole

Bang! It was too late. The door behind me slammed shut as I stepped into the mysterious room. Although it was the afternoon, it was pitch-black. Cautiously I turned round and tried to look for the light switch. Instead of finding a switch, I found a hole, a hole big enough to look through. Slowly I bent down to look through the hole, terrified of what was on the other side. Suddenly, a hand with long, dirty nails gripped my throat like a knife stabbing my skin. I let out my last, piercing scream...

Maryam Bint Idris (12)
Jaamiatul Imaam Muhammad Zakaria School, Bradford

Basement Horror

I always knew I'd never get out of trouble easily. Cassy and I were playing around whilst the demonic teacher, Mrs Charles, was watching us. She pinched us firmly and dragged us down the creaky, wooden stairs which lead to the school basement. It was damp and cold. Chains were covered in dried blood. Crumbling skeletons lay there peacefully. All I could imagine down there was the yelps and cries from the innocent children suffering the pain in the basement. Mrs Charles left us down there and she locked the door. Faint growling came from the other end. 'Help!'

Imaan Mahmood (11)

Jaamiatul Imaam Muhammad Zakaria School, Bradford

The Cave's Revenge

I knew Tom was hiding in the cave. I couldn't bear it. Skipping merrily into the cave, the door slammed. 'Argh!' I shrieked. 'Tom, Tom?' I whispered. I knew it was too late. Cautiously I tiptoed forward and finally found Tom. 'Tom!' I screamed with happiness. 'I've found you!' Suddenly, a huge dark shadow approached behind me. 'Tom, help me!' I shouted. Tom's body was hanging on the wall, blood dripped down onto his feet. His hands were covered in sweat. His eyes turned red. I knew it wasn't Tom. I knew the devious devil had killed him...

Umme-Imaan Khan (11)

Jaamiatul Imaam Muhammad Zakaria School, Bradford

Waiting There...

You better be careful because it gets closer every second. You can't see it but it's there, just waiting to choose its next prey. It could be lurking near your window or outside your door. Or maybe, just maybe, right behind you. It springs up anywhere, any time. It could strike right now but don't worry, it eventually goes to everyone. It likes an open body, so wear a coat and scarf when you go out on a chilly day. It mostly goes up your nose, then *atchoo!* That's when you've got the cold.

Moral: Stay warm in the winter.

Asma Rawat (12)
Jaamiatul Imaam Muhammad Zakaria School, Bradford

Stalker

Have you ever wondered what it's like to walk down a deserted street 100% sure that you're going to die any moment? Now! It all began when I was invited to a spooky Halloween party. As I was on my way home, my friends and I were walking down the silent, gloomy street. All of a sudden I had a strange vision that I was being watched, followed by someone smelly and very terrifying. The next moment, my vision had a knife. I turned round the deserted street and heard a voice say, 'I want to kill you...'

Maariya Kayat (12)
Jaamiatul Imaam Muhammad Zakaria School, Bradford

The Hot, Delicious, Mysterious World

An empty, spooky, round world resting in peace. Suddenly, a noise began. It caused a blast, with steam that shook like an earthquake. In a flash the bright light shone like the sun. The volcano tipped and filled the whole world with lava. Snowballs fell from the heavens which melted far into the Underworld. A long, thin, metal finger reached into the world which spun round and round. The whole world dropped deep into my hole. 'Ouch! It's too hot, Mum!' I shouted.

Fiza Ilyas (13)
Jaamiatul Imaam Muhammad Zakaria School, Bradford

The Baby Leopard

I was walking through the big, green, shiny leaves and bushes of the forest when I saw a little baby leopard. This was strange and creepy. As I went near it, I realised it was in a mini Moses basket. It looked at me and kept his tail still. I went closer and closer until we were face-to-face. It stroked my arm with its soft, fluffy paws. Suddenly, I heard 'Rooaarr!' I quickly ran without making a sound and hid behind a tree. I shivered with a tingly feeling and ran for my life back home!

Haafizah Khanom (13)
Jaamiatul Imaam Muhammad Zakaria School, Bradford

Midnight

The clock struck midnight. I was face to face with the devil of the past. I looked left, then right! What shall I do? Will I live or die? Suddenly, I felt something grab my back. I looked back, it was the soul of my friend smiling strangely. The Devil took out his pitchfork. Then he put it near my neck and stared at me for a while. But what did I do? I woke up in the middle of my science lesson, realising my brain had travelled to another destination.

Ume-Ruaqia Zia (13)

Jaamiatul Imaam Muhammad Zakaria School, Bradford

The Forked Tongue

I walked faster and faster, it was getting dark. I didn't even know where I was going. I walked slowly on the empty path that lead up to an abandoned park. An elderly lady was coming out, she stopped and her eyes followed me walking. She was wearing a leather jacket. As she smiled I saw a forked tongue flick from her mouth. I ran and ran faster through the park. My heart pounding like a drum. I saw a shadow loom over me from the dim light. I was knocked sideways. My eyes opened slightly. I saw a forked tongue...

Zainab Daya (13)

Jaamiatul Imaam Muhammad Zakaria School, Bradford

A Dark Light

I saw a bright light in the distance. It was really bright. It wasn't a lit up candle, it was something else. I wasn't scared of anything, in fact I'm the bravest in my school. So I walked up to the abandoned elementary school part of the cemetery. I heard a blood-curdling screech. But I couldn't have. It was impossible. It sounded like a voice from the unseen, someone or something being dragged by the roots to the darkest part of Hell with the sins of his ignorant followers. Something that made me loudly howl.

Fatimah Iqbal (11)
Jaamiatul Imaam Muhammad Zakaria School, Bradford

I'm A Werewolf

It was a dark, shadowy night. The wind whispered the calls of the dead. Temptation rushed through me, touching every nerve and a part of me kept saying, 'Go!' It was too hard to resist. I went outside, my breath echoed in the silence. I looked towards the bright moonlit sky, pain hit me and darkness rushed through my veins. It was visible on me. I howled in pain and was on all fours. I was feeling a macabre hunger. I opened my eyes hearing heavy breathing, then I realised the beast I'd become. A creature. A monster. A werewolf.

Aishah Ismail Rawat (13)
Jaamiatul Imaam Muhammad Zakaria School, Bradford

Fried Fish

Dark and brutal, I was cramped in a small basket. I could smell a sour odour filling my nostrils, when suddenly someone grabbed me, squeezing my body tight. I was put under the icy-cold water. Unable to breathe, I was then slammed onto a wooden plank. I heard a sharp knife being pulled out of its case. Tiptoe... The sound was getting louder and louder and closer and closer. My heartbeat accelerated. *Slit!* My lungs burst out, squeezing my juice everywhere. I was carelessly tossed into a black pan sizzling with oil. It was too late.

Rafia Hussain (13)
Jaamiatul Imaam Muhammad Zakaria School, Bradford

The Flash Of Darkness

As I walked towards my house it felt as if someone or something was following me. I opened the door slowly. The door creaked. In a flash of darkness, I walked in. *Bang!* The door shut behind me. I turned around trying to open the door but it was locked. I could hear noises coming towards the living room. I walked towards the room, nothing was there. I sat down. I saw the same flash of darkness go past. I could hear giggling. I looked under the sofa and what did I see? My cheeky little sister laughing!

Raisah Tabassum Ahmed (12)
Jaamiatul Imaam Muhammad Zakaria School, Bradford

There I Was...

There I was going for a stroll in the forest. Suddenly, it started following, then chasing me. It was white and had black eyes, a mouthful of blood and hands filled with blood. It followed, then chased me until I came to a clifftop. Just before I fell, it gave a cackle and a bloody hand reached out and saved me from falling! Then that hand pulled off the whiteness to reveal my friend Daisy. 'What are you doing?' I asked.
'Scaring you with a bed sheet, buttoned eyes, red lipstick and red inked hands!' They both laughed out loud.

Misbah Shaikh (12)
Jaamiatul Imaam Muhammad Zakaria School, Bradford

What Was That?

It began when I forgot something at school. I ran and reached the school doors; as I was knocking, someone locked the school gates. *What was that? I'm trapped,* I thought to myself. Suddenly, the wind started howling and the school windows opened. Shadows appeared in every window. From one window something came out. It dragged me along the school pitch. I started screaming, 'Get off me! Who are you?' It left marks all over my back.
After a while I heard a voice saying, 'You're doomed! Happy Halloween!' Bob's excited voice reached my ears.
'What were you thinking, Bob?'

Rumaithah Iffat (12)
Jaamiatul Imaam Muhammad Zakaria School, Bradford

They're Gone

They set off through the woods trying to find anything that could possibly be a clue. One of them at the back suddenly dropped his riddle and just disappeared. Another dropped his piece of the puzzle and just disappeared. Another dropped her piece of paper and disappeared. The last person just dropped to the floor dead.

An hour later a posse of eight adults who were shouting for their kids walked along the path, which was twisting and turning just like their stomachs, looking for children that never came home.

Hope Abigail Sefton (11)

Notre Dame High School, Sheffield

Wil O' The Wisp: Mist Wraith

The mist creeps through the trees making them shiver. The gaping pool of water is sheltered by the canopy of witches' fingers. I am here, you cannot see me. I am falling, but never moving. I am not dead, but I'm never alive. Call me all you like, I will not hear you. Scream, shout and curse the state of this world, but your cries will fall on deaf ears. The answers you seek are secrets from the end of time. The questions you ask are from the dawn of time and they will never be revealed.

Rachel Jones (14)

Notre Dame High School, Sheffield

The Unknown Name

Cautiously, I crept like a child in the middle of the night sneaking candy from the kitchen. Clouds swiftly moved as if being chased. Towering trees and evergreen bushes whispered in consternation. From the corner of my eye, I could see a strange gravestone carved with a familiar name... a worrying name. Twirling branches clung together in anxiety. Black crows talked amongst each other in their mysterious language. I continued to walk. Now I know the name...

Mufaro Chikwanha (11)
Notre Dame High School, Sheffield

The Unmarked Headstone

A girl walked across a graveyard, the icy air tickling her nose, as she plodded through the sticky mud. Twilight shone down, she could hardly see as she moved through the cemetery. In one numb hand she held a red poppy. Her black raven hair flew up with the wind. She stopped beside an unmarked grave. Her violet eyes glared at the headstone that had plagued her family for centuries. 'The curse ends tonight!' she cried, as she dived into the grave. A scream was heard that night. All they found was a bloodstained headstone and a poppy...

Thandie Grant (13)
Notre Dame High School, Sheffield

Torture

He was tied down with a crimson rope. He was stuck. His one, blue eye darted around in its socket; as if looking for escape but there was none. He tried to get out, knowing what would come for him. He jerked around, tormented by the blood-curdling screams that ripped through his ears. But then... The screams stopped. The man left, the body dropped. A man came in, two men went out, one draped with a snow-white cloth. He was sat down. He was tied down. He was stuck. The rope deep red and sticky...

Owen Wright (11)

Notre Dame High School, Sheffield

The Forgotten One

A woman walked through the gloomy corridor. The blood banks rattled as she passed dragging her legs behind her. The bags under her eyes grew heavier and heavier, she dreamed of her awaiting bed, but suddenly a crash! She shivered in agony. What seemed like a never-ending pain struck her body. In her last few precious seconds, she looked up and glared into the eyes of her killer. Open wounds were across her face. His smile was oppressive. You see, this is what killed her, not the blood gushing from her body.

Oliver O'Brien (11)

Notre Dame High School, Sheffield

The Locket

Tumbleweed rolled across the shifting dunes. A line of footprints led across the sand towards the worn stone. She stepped forwards, trembling as she undid the clasp on the locket. Her eye glinted, showing the tiniest hint of fear on her otherwise expressionless face. Reluctantly, she tipped the contents of the tiny locket onto the ancient stone block. Instantly, inky black tendrils swarmed from the locket, wrapping around her, engulfing her. She was screaming, crying, pleading and the locket was rattling, shaking and she screamed for the last time – silence. Tumbleweed rolled across the shifting dunes.

Molly Gore (11)

Notre Dame High School, Sheffield

Missty

One school trip was going to be fun... Hospital 11.00. Dark clouds surround depression on the hospital. So, me and my 'friends' will have the best day... There's no adults now... No light, no happiness. Just fright. 'Guys, no!'

17.00: 'Argh!'- as a girl cried, me and two girls ran towards her. Blood splattered against the wall. Her chest was open and her eyes were bleeding.

22.00: Someone blew out our candle. We lit it back. One girl was hanging and being choked by a rope. She laughed, then cried. Was she the murderer? No... it was me – Missty. 'Why?'

Austeja Janusaite (12)

Notre Dame High School, Sheffield

The Dark Forest

Through the dark, in the dead forest, where no one was brave enough to go. Windy sat with a million thoughts fallowing her. Thoughts of what's going to happen to her; thoughts of what her family would be feeling; thoughts of how she was going to die. She tried to stop thinking, but how? She was blaming herself for getting lost in the forest. Windy was fed up and feeling confused. 'This is ridiculous,' she whispered. She was worried. She was scared. She was terrified. Windy ran and ran into the unknown... Would she find her way out?

Taif Al-Naumani (12)
Sheffield Springs Academy, Sheffield

Hospital Visit

Hospital visit; Mr B was going to the hospital, his hand was stuck in a teapot. He was sat next to a lady who was in a wheelchair and was strapped up in bandages. Mr B did all these things; moving his hand, turning it around; wiggling his fingers... The nurse said, '23?' Mr B looked at his paper and he had 76. Everyone was laughing just because his hand was stuck in the teapot. The lady sat next to Mr B was laughing and Mr B looked at her ticket, 25. When she wasn't looking, he swapped them!

Christivie Fernandes (11)
Sheffield Springs Academy, Sheffield

Detention

She wasn't there. As soon as we walked in, we were expecting a bellow of anger. We didn't hear a sound of rage. We could hear a pin drop. Then a shadow raced across the corridor. *Clip-clop, clip-clop* went the high-heels of the short-tempered, angry teacher, sounding like the cracking of a whip. Her grey-stained hair and her long pointy chin. Her long, thin arms with razor-sharp nails. She stood tall in front of us. This wasn't going to be pleasant.

Joe Goulding (11)
Tapton School, Sheffield

Witnessing Death

Trembling towards the dilapidated house, the gloomy night closed in on me. My heart started to pound. Screams approached from the house! Trapped! Nowhere to go! Nowhere... the house took me. *Slam!* I heard the sound of a chainsaw. Something dropped onto my arm... blood. Fright slithered down my back! I felt the room spinning, and like the walls were chasing me. I scrunched myself together and I began to see an unclear figure. Sudden heavy breathing trembled down my neck. The sound of a chainsaw rang again. I stared into its eyes. I witnessed death!

Sam Oakley (11)
Tapton School, Sheffield

Where Am I?

A damp mist hung in the air, I wouldn't make it before dark. Rain poured down rapidly. I needed to get shelter. I saw an abandoned garage ahead. 'I'll go inside and call Dad.' When I went in the garage, all I could see was cobwebs, hanging from the ceiling. The door slammed behind me; dust fell. I heard footsteps! But what could it be? A shadow *slipped*. 'Who's there?' I whispered. No answer. My heart was thundering. I blundered through the dark. My breath was fast, shallow, trembling. Without warning, an icy hand gripped my shoulder.

Emad Abouelrish (11)
Tapton School, Sheffield

Death Of The Night

As Simon walked home from a tiring day at work, he felt a cold-blooded shadow peer over his shoulder. He felt an unstable breath on the side of his neck. A shiver came from Simon's trembling body. Simon took a deep breath and turned around. He jumped backwards. But no one was there. He carried on walking with a scared step. *Splash!* the puddle went, as Simon stumbled into it. He looked at his wet foot. 'Argh!' A zombie flew out of his foot, taking a great bite. To the ground he went, blood everywhere. He was dead.

Elana Ashton (12)
Tapton School, Sheffield

The Figure

Despite my map I was lost in a wood. The sun had run away. Suddenly, my ears picked up to the sound of rustling in the bushes. 'Help!' I screamed. Something launched at me. The force of it crashing into me made me stumble backwards. What was it? It was feathery and small. Phew! It was only a bird. Sweat poured down my face. My head darted back and forth. A figure appeared; I looked closely. It had no nose, one eye and really sharp teeth. Suddenly, it was behind me. That was the last time anyone saw me!

Sam Carré (12)
Tapton School, Sheffield

Silence...

I stood there, staring into the night sky. A deafening scream pierced my ears. The park fell silent. The swing was going back and forth... back and forth. My face was burning, my hands were shaking. Sounds of death echoed around me. I placed my hand on the swing. 'Stop!' she shrieked. A pale veiny hand grabbed my wrist. Thoughts of terror danced in my head.
'You shall always remember tonight,' she whispered. *Clip, clip.* Sounds of scissors came closer and closer. I saw it. Fire was burning in her eyes. Was this the end?

Emily Bidder (11)
Tapton School, Sheffield

Taken By The Zombies

Arriving at the airport, I shivered as I watched the rush to leave. I heard that the last plane was boarding. Within seconds the planes were all gone and it was as if the airport had been abandoned for years! I stepped out of the airport. Looking around I saw an opening. Damn! I was too late, there were zombies flooding in, I stumbled backwards. With my trembling hands I reached behind me for the door, grabbing the handle I realised I was too late, it was locked. Now all I could do was wait.

Hannah MacPherson (11)

Tapton School, Sheffield

The Little Girl

There I was, in the middle of life and death. I placed my hand on the cold, rusty door handle. That's when I heard a blood-curdling scream pierce the silence of the asylum. I wasn't alone. Despite all the nightmares going through my head, I still searched. The air became tense as I walked into a dark, gloomy room. From the corner of my eye, I saw a reflection shimmering from behind the dusty curtain. A mirror. And that is when I saw her.
'I've been waiting for you.'
I turned around. Little did I know that was the end.

Megan Romano (12)

Tapton School, Sheffield

The Terrifying Twins

I was alone in the abandoned school. The shadows of the trees cast over me. While the wind danced through the town. The windows and the doors where boarded up. Just then I heard a creak of a door and it opened. I thought I was alone, but maybe not. I walked into the classroom and on the whiteboard was: 'Come play with me'. I ran; I was terrified. Despite being spooked, I stopped. I looked around then I saw them. They were twins, 'Come play with us!' they screeched. Then they grabbed me. Never to be seen again.

Alissia Dunn (11)

Tapton School, Sheffield

Shadows

Bang! The sound of the door echoed through the derelict asylum. Dust particles floated around as if it was scared of something. Little did she know she walked into her own deathtrap. *Drip, drip, drip.* She knew something was behind her but she didn't know what. Her breath contaminated the air as she walked closer to the darkness. A breath grazed her face, it was warm but *dead*, she slowly turned around and a look of horror swept her face. At that moment, she knew her time had come. A spine-chilling scream echoed then the asylum was *silent...*

Shiffa Gamal (11)

Tapton School, Sheffield

Knock, Knock...

Knock, knock. Curiosity filled her mind. Slowly, she pushed her warm duvet off her and slipped out of bed. Beneath her feet, the floorboard creaked. No one was at the door. She sighed. She was sure she had heard a knock. *Knock, knock.* It was real. It wasn't coming from the door! Quickly, she tiptoed back to her bedroom. It was louder now. *Knock. Hiss.* Her head turned to the mirror. It glowed. 'Come closer,' it whispered, 'come to me!' Cautiously, she placed her fingertip on its surface. Little did she know that this was the end...

Yakin Belkhir (11)

Tapton School, Sheffield

Lost In The Unknown

My hand closed on the handle. I was shaking, sweating and terrified. Pounding, my heart was racing as fast as a cheetah. My hair danced in the wind. My fingers were turning to blocks of ice in this inhumane weather. I had spotted the church as I was wandering (completely lost) in the woods. Turning around, I stared hard at the isolated woods; I was looking for the impossible signs of life. I did not hear the thick steel door scrape open. Suddenly, shivers bolted down my spine as something cold grabbed my shoulder, yanking me into the unknown...

Ben Atkinson (11)

Tapton School, Sheffield

Municipality

First London, then Asia and soon the rest of the world. Leaving just New Zealand left – but they were coming for us. I had to prepare, I knew a place that could get me everything to survive; not knowing when they'd come I got my dad's hunting rifle and waited! *Bang...* I was woken by panic, I opened the front door to find chaos, people dead everywhere killed by panicking people! Fog came oozing into the street like fingers of a monster. A missile, it was the end, *boom!* I thought they were dead; but out of the fire, zombies!

William Stobbs (11)

Tapton School, Sheffield

Walk Home

Dark, cold dim. The wind blew though my fingertips. Frost shivered down my back. I was walking home, alone. The small avenues turned into tiresome motorways, I looked down at my watch 3.30. It can't be, I left school at 3.30, I lifted my head and glared at the gennel. This type of road always confused me, down or across? I slid my foot down but in my gut I knew it was wrong. The gennel was cold, bitter. I tiptoed into the darkness. Then I took my last breath...

Alexandria Sagripanti (11)

Tapton School, Sheffield

The Dentist

I stepped foot in the dentist, the crackle of the wind, the shadow of the drill. The light breathing of what I thought was a human. The old dentist sat quietly waiting for them, like a snake waiting for his prey ready to strike. I edged to the creepy door handle, I lay my hand on the eerie doorknob. I walked towards one of the rooms. Suddenly, something shuffled behind me. Then I realised I was trapped. The old creepy dentist at one end with the drill and twins at the other, I was trapped.

Tom Herbert (12)
Tapton School, Sheffield

Detention

For hours my legs had been filling with pins and needles. As I stumbled out from the torture, I stamped on the floor hoping the pain would drift away. As the bang echoed around the deserted hallway, a deafening scream pierced through me. The lights flickered off. I followed a faint light to a classroom. I placed my fingertips on the handle and pushed. Locked. I looked behind me. Nothing. As I started to run, a hand grabbed my arm. I looked down. A knife. The pain was unbearable. I tried to move, but I couldn't. It was too late.

Gracie May Tierney-Kitchener (11)
Tapton School, Sheffield

Mirrored

Mia froze. The unhinged door of the dilapidated house lay on the floor. One step and it would be done. Taking a breath, she entered. Then something entranced her. A dust caked, gilded, golden mirror stood in the hall. Hypnotised, she approached it, every step sending shudders around her. Suits of armour glared at her from the shadows. She had arrived. Hand shaking, she wiped away the dust. There was her reflection, with one big difference, there was a hole in her torso. Terrified, she took a step back. Her reflection stepped forward out of the mirror, holding an axe...

Isaac Hale (11)

Tapton School, Sheffield

Pain-Infested Screams

The floorboards creaked as I entered the room. Her pale pink tongue wiping the knife clean of blood, just about avoiding slicing it off. Her head slowly twisted around to face me. The rumours were true! Her eyes had glazed over, blood was splattered all over her. The silver knife glinted in the bright moonlight as she rose it up into the air. She took a step and I took one back. It happened in a blink of an eye; she quickly plunged the knife deep into my heart, twisting it round, not caring about my pain-infested screams.

Honor Duffy (11)

Tapton School, Sheffield

The Institution

I was lost. Lost in the gaze of cruel eyes. Sadistic screams came through the walls of terror as I walked upon the bloodstained floors of the mental institution. I continued to walk down the corridor, trembling with every step. I stopped. A horrifying sight appeared in my eyes. A short figure appeared. Blood stained her uniform, name tag; *nurse!* She came closer. She raised her knife above her head. Suddenly, lightning struck and my torch cut out. She was right in front of me. Suddenly, I fell. My last sight on Earth was her mangled face...

Will Locker (12)

Tapton School, Sheffield

Once Upon A Torture

Despite the signs of death that were echoing around me, and the nails piercing out of the ground, I still felt the thrill, to enter, the doll's house... I went up to the grand house and read the sign: *House For Girls*, painted in red. 'Come play with me,' it seemed to whisper. Suddenly, I thought I heard the real thing – a doll! Standing there staring, I dropped down to the ground...

I woke up and I felt cold, I looked up. The dolls were playing, pulling the chains attached to me; pulling harder, their faces showing sadism.

Lois Anna Steele Blake (12)

Tapton School, Sheffield

The Mysterious House

In complete darkness, I slowly stepped towards the abandoned house. The steps creaked as though they were going to snap in half any second. My hand trembled with shock. Dilemma thoughts were whizzing round in my head: *Should I open it? What if I get locked in?* In the end I decided to take a look. The door swung open eerily, so fast it nearly broke. I took two steps in and the door slammed behind me violently. Suddenly, I realised I wasn't alone... As I looked up, I saw some piercing eyes staring right at me...

Sasha Narraway (12)
Tapton School, Sheffield

The Phone Call In The Woods

I entered the eerie forest, I heard a phone ringing. I looked down, I saw it, I was petrified to pick up the phone and answer it, I didn't know whose phone it was. I overcome my fear and answered. 'Hello?' I said. 'Who is it?'
All the person said was, 'Look up.' I looked up and all I saw was a person whose head had been chopped off. He said, 'You have twenty minutes to get a bag in the house in front of you or the same will happen to everyone you love!'

Abdul Malek Ahmed Abuserwal (11)
Tapton School, Sheffield

Point Final

I reached the end of the forest, I stared back toward it... The thing, red eyes locked onto mine burning my soul, my essence. I heard a chime, a bell. I had reached it, the school, it was closed. I stepped on something, it was an AK-47. I tried to pick it up, I fell it was so heavy. Finally, I picked it up, there was a note: 'You'll need it'. I walked into the maze of corridors. A scream! Suddenly, a thing jumped at me, eyes glowing I blasted it to Hell.

Abdul-Haseeb Usman (12)

Tapton School, Sheffield

Terror

I was lost. I couldn't let him find me. My lamp died hours ago and I was his next victim. As I crept down the pitch-black tunnel I realised all hope was lost. Each step I took seemed to go in the wrong direction. Was there a way out of this endless labyrinth? All of a sudden, he was there! The hideous, green monster leapt at me, missing by an inch. I turned and I ran as fast as I could. The ground disappeared beneath me and I was falling, falling and then it went black...

Will Szollosy (12)

Tapton School, Sheffield

Button Eyes

Despite it being a dark, gloomy night, Damien being as daring as he was, still travelled to the old abandoned house like he planned. Alone! He slowly stepped out of the jeep he was driving, anxious for what was ahead of him. Was it even his jeep? A winter's breeze brushed his pale face as he stepped towards the mansion. It for some reason didn't feel quite right to Damien. A strange figure stared at him through one of the windows with black button eyes. As he walked forward he felt a strange feeling on his shoulder. 'Welcome.'

Alex Welch-Maas (11)
Tapton School, Sheffield

The Shining Leprodog

As I walked through the haunted forest, fog started to merge with darkness. Guilt rushed down my veins! My gigantic brain was being erased. Bravely walking, I hesitated. Tentatively I screamed! Its bright yellow eyes looked down my black soul. It stared back! As its eyes turned white, it got struck by lightning, it became a dog. A leprodog! It took me to a farm where the farmer questioned my sudden appearance. The dog approached. Suddenly, it vanished! He said, 'A dog, could it be the wizard's dog that died in a spell! I wonder!'

Abdul-Malik Ibrahim (11)
Tapton School, Sheffield

It

I picked up a camera which had a video. *Tick-tock,* the clock struck nine, a young man was running. He kept saying, 'It is coming.' *Tick-tock,* the clock struck ten, the camera started to blur, I saw it, the little girl! She was singing, 'You will die when the clock strikes twelve.' He started to run. He found an abandoned house. *Tick-tock,* the clock struck eleven. He picked up a gun and ran outside. He shot the little girl in the chest. She was standing.

The video ended, I ran and ran and ran. *Tick-tock,* it was twelve...

Yusuf Shakir Mohamoud (11)

Tapton School, Sheffield

Click, Click, Slide Goes Legless Mental

I can hear it but I can't see it. Its crackling breath echoes through the endless rooms around the deserted asylum. Despite the horror racing into my head, I still search. I see a steamed window, it's cloudy with breath. Whose breath? I can hear her nails digging into the floors, one hand at a time. *Click, click, slide.* It pulls itself towards me. I race into a damp room. Its nails screech as they run down the steel door. 'Let me in!' it croaks. I can see a pair of feet. I pull them. I've found its legs...

Alice Goddard (11)

Tapton School, Sheffield

The Dracaenae

Fog seeped into the room; creeping in like a smokey creature of darkness, she huddled in dusty crumbling corner. The worn, derelict building tottered precariously. Their hissing voices echoed in the distance, seeming to get louder. 'They know I'm here,' she whispered. Turning, she ran across the weather-worn ruins. The hiss of the snake-woman approached. The footsteps behind her quickened. Stumbling through the decaying doorway of one of the more intact ruins. She retreated into the wall, her heart thudding against her chest as her pursuers came in and bared their fangs at her. There was no escape.

Hannah Adeni (11)

Tapton School, Sheffield

Soul Survivor

It felt like an eternity. An endless horror of rotting arms was hanging off the lifeless and still bodies. Despite being scared, Alex ran on. In the street, it was worse... More bodies and corpses were just sitting there. Unable to help, Alex slumped down by a derelict house and began to cry. It was all his fault. He had caused the apocalypse and now was the only one left. His parents had been the first to go. After that it had been his little sister. Suddenly, he heard a blood-curdling groan from a shadowy figure who was approaching him...

Ethan Marchment (12)

Tapton School, Sheffield

Monster

As I carefully moved my way through the golden leaves, I felt as if a pair of eyes were watching me. My heart pounded. Shadows kept on popping up everywhere which made my anxiety a whole lot worse. Was I hallucinating or not? Suddenly, I heard a crumpling in the leaves. Quickly, I turned around and got my weapon, my phone. I dialled 999, I didn't want to die. All of a sudden, I overheard an eerie moan. I shook with fear as I edged away. Just then, a large horrifying thing appeared. I screamed!

Noor-Ulhuda Aldbrez (11)
Tapton School, Sheffield

What's Your Name?

As she picked up the ringing phone, she heard a thunder crash at the window. 'Hello?'
'Hello! What's your name?' a creaky, bone-chilling voice said.
'Why do you want to know?'
'So I know who I'm about to kill!' *Crash!* He broke in, she let out a blood-curdling scream and ran upstairs. He chased her. She threw a chair at him, but he dodged. Despite the fact the girl was slow, she beat him to her room, locked the old door and called the police. Her phone died. 'I'm coming for you.' He barged in and raised his bloody knife...

Samuel Meekings (11)
Tapton School, Sheffield

The Forest Demon

'Argh!' The high-pitched screech rocked the forest. The beast was almost upon him, bearing down with paranormal speed. 'Help, somebody help!' he yelled. That was the last thing he ever said! He was dead!

James had decided to investigate the forest at night. Little did he know it would be a fatal mistake. Suddenly, he heard a blood-curdling scream and though petrified, decided to investigate.

There was a dead body lying on the path in front of James. The body was as pale as a ghost. It had two bite marks on its neck. The beast spied its next prey.

Thomas Chamberlain (12)
Tapton School, Sheffield

Alone!

A dilapidated, derelict house. On my own. The wind was howling and thick fog was beginning to settle. Rain was pounding on the windows and echoing through the dull, empty house. Suddenly, a thundering sound alarmed me. My parents? I was scared. Frightened. Was it my parents? My heart was pounding as fast as a stampeding cheetah. Slowly, I put my hand out. Shaking with fear, I opened the door. It wasn't my parents, they were people I had never seen before. They reached out at me with their dirty rotten fingers, I screamed...

Kady Harris (11)
Tapton School, Sheffield

Death In The Dark

I just wanted to curl up and die because all I knew right now was nothing. As I dragged myself through the mud, clawing at the ground with fog and mist all around me, I heard a blood-curdling scream breaking the silence of the forest! Realising it was my own petrified voice at the dark creatures falling from the purple-bruised sky, I started to run, run for my life even though I was in so much pain. The next thing I saw was darkness. Just creepy darkness. Something cut my throat and pain took over my whole body... then nothingness!

Hebe Hope (12)

Tapton School, Sheffield

The Doll

Walking into the woods, I saw an abandoned house. My spine tingled as I opened the door. I hear a creak, my heart beat stopped. As I walked down the corridor, the pictures were staring at me like people in agony. There was one room that was calling my name. I looked back and the walls were closing in, I had to get out. I got out in the nick of time, but there was a doll staring at me.

Mason Russell (11)

Tapton School, Sheffield

Hell House

I was home alone with my two sisters. It was my first time alone. Suddenly, the radio turned on, it sounded fuzzy. Soon as I took a step the TV turned on, the words on the TV said, 'I'm coming for you!' Suddenly, I ran upstairs and went into my sister's room, they were not there. All I saw was a doll sitting on a rocking chair with a blood-covered knife in its hand. As soon as I was about to scream I noticed blood coming from the wardrobe, then the doll was gone...

Daniel Garcia (12)

Tapton School, Sheffield

The Forest

As he trembled through the deep, dark woods, his feet crunched on the autumn leaves. Owls were hooting and trees were swooshing as the wind blew through the blood-curdling forest. Walking round every corner his five senses came to life.

After hours of walking in the forest he came into a tree that had fallen over and blocked his path. Trapped. Stuck. Nowhere to go.

Leo Chappell (12)

Tapton School, Sheffield

Lost

As I woke up, I was trembling vigorously. I had no idea where I was or how I got there, but I certainly wasn't home. Lying on the stone-cold floor, I scanned the dark, gloomy area. I saw heavily reinforced doors with rusty metal flaps. *Clip-clop, clip-clop.* I felt heavy footsteps. Standing up carefully, I felt cold sweat trickle down my spine. Walking slowly around the area, I heard the footsteps nearing. *Dash!* As quick as a knife, a shadow of a figure slipped across the wall. I stopped. I felt something sharp sink deep into my leg.

Ali Merza (11)

Tapton School, Sheffield

A Wander In The Woods

As I stumbled through the intimidating woods, a chill crept up my spine. Silence was deafening me, making my heart pound louder than a gunshot, piecing the air. *Snap!* I froze in my place, despite wanting to turn round, I was paralysed with fear.

Racing through the never-ending maze of towering trees, I had lost all bearings of the land around me. I stopped and gazed into the gloomy forest; I wondered whether I would ever wake up from this nightmare. I was alone, just me and the darkness, or so I thought...

Scarlett Berwick Clephan (11)

Tapton School, Sheffield

The Creature In The Murky Woods

As Rachel walked through the woods, looking around every couple of paces, she felt as though someone was watching her. Suddenly, she heard a twig snapping behind her and she looked quickly over her shoulder. She felt a hand close over her mouth and another hand close over her wrist. Then the figure started to drag her away through the woods...

Charlotte Hampton (11)
Tapton School, Sheffield

Murder House

I walked into the house through the broken chipped, old door frame as the door slowly creaked open. I put the boxes that I was carrying on the floor and walked into the kitchen. There was a knife on the floor, it was dripping with blood. A shiver ran down my spine and I heard a loud bang in the basement. I walked down the eerie stairs until I reached the basement. I walked through the different rooms on the cold, stone floor. I turned around, I heard something behind me. I carried on walking. Suddenly, someone grabbed my mouth...

Asha Spruce (12)
Tapton School, Sheffield

Waiting By The Blade

Dancing, fiery embers illuminated the scarce woods. Despite the killer on the lose, the suicidal girl waited. When you go down in the woods today, you better not go alone. The tune rang in her ear. Suddenly, she heard a whisper, 'I can wait with you.' A cold blade slid across her throat. Unable to scream, she laid in a pool of blood, the singing in her ear. She recalled the knife in and out and a smile. As always he had a smile as he ran away into the dark and murderous night for his next victim... You.

Sarah Abdul-Rub (11)

Tapton School, Sheffield

Death!

Bang! I slammed the rustic door behind me as I stumbled through the deserted village. I ran for my life, as if Death was chasing me. I stopped, my heart pounding. I slumped down against the old crumbling gravestone in the moonlight. Leaves scattered around the graves in the wind. Unexpectedly everything went silent. My ears were shocked by a piercing scream, then breath on the back of my neck, followed by a cold, bony hand on my shoulder... I was stabbed! I fell to the floor; blood surrounding me...

Eve Willis (11)

Tapton School, Sheffield

The Last Step

Despite the fact that my tyre was punctured in the middle of the woods, I had my phone so I wasn't worried. Argh! No signal! No way out of this place, my only option was to go into the woods and find someone to help me get home. So I kept on going through the woods. *Boom!* Lightning hitting the trees, rain falling down my head, felt like it was going to fall off. There were lights in front of my eyes, I ran up to the lights, it was a house. I opened the door, nothing there. *Bang!*

Cam Delaney (11)
Tapton School, Sheffield

The Mysterious House

Despite the house looking dilapidated, my determination dragged me even closer. Suddenly, the rusty door opened. My heart pounded. With curiosity rushing through me, I stepped in...
As I shouted, 'Anyone in?' Silence continued. Until... a ghostly voice echoed around me like a blast of misty wind. I could feel the tension running through my veins!
With me breathing heavily, my head looking 360 degrees... something appeared! It disappeared at the speed of light.

Hasini Liyanage (12)
Tapton School, Sheffield

The Monster

One dark, stormy night I suddenly woke up to a loud snapping sound, then leaves were rustling like someone was out there. When I mustered the courage to go and look outside there was nothing there but a field mouse. Then I heard it again, a loud snapping noise so I went downstairs and it was a big, enormous, green monster. Its skin was rotten and its eyes were red and it had fire all over its body.

Matthew Sanderson (11)
Tapton School, Sheffield

Simply Demonic

Pain. That's all my mind registered, that and a high-pitched cackle. No normal person could make that sound, even a computer couldn't create a noise so sinister. Managing to access my surroundings, I realised I was in a cage. How satanic. A chainsaw, that's all I heard and then she appeared. She's always haunted me, stalked my home like prey, leaving me devilish messages. Despite this, I never panicked; I had no reason to until now. *Now I've done it*, I thought, *flirted with death, danced with the Devil*. Now I'd have to face the barbaric, demonic consequences.

Amanda Mercier (12)
Tapton School, Sheffield

The Figure

I stumbled as I sprinted through the eerie blackness. It had seemed a good idea in the daylight but now I was scared. I looked around; all I could see was trees and darkness. The trees stood tall and forbidding like iron bars; trapping me in. A twig snapped behind me. I bolted like a cheetah. I caught a glimpse of the tall murderous figure. I kept running until I could run no more. Even then I kept running, running for my life. I stopped and turned around. He was there. That was the last thing I remembered.

Ben Fuller (11)
Tapton School, Sheffield

Where Now?

Here I was again, alone in this abandoned warehouse. I've never been outside. I wouldn't dare to. A howling sound shot a hated tingle down my spine. What if it comes again? I'm terrified. I hate this place; I want to go. Those sounds, those stupid sounds. Are they just in my head? I don't know. It's all happening too quickly. My hand is trembling, I can hear the windows shudder. That was where it was last. In the window. What if it takes me away this time? I can see it! It's coming again. 'No! Stop! Stop!'

Haval Mahmud (11)
Tapton School, Sheffield

The Blood Tree

A piercing scream shook the woods and drilled into my eardrums. Running forwards, I tripped on a root of one of the crooked trees. Owls hooted in the branches of the trees. A frosty wind whipped past me, leaving me chilled to the bone. I had to get away from them. Despite the fact that it was dark, I made out the simple outline of a tree with a massive cut in it. I stopped; it looked as if someone or something had made it. I turned my torch on. Instead of being clear, the sap was blood red...

Srinanda Chakraborty (11)

Tapton School, Sheffield

Haunted

Slowly Tim advanced towards the door, not knowing someone was watching him. *Bang!* He fell down some stairs, hearing noises in front and behind him. Standing up, he felt someone breathing on him, hesitating, he turned around, nothing. Tim continued his journey down a long hallway looking from left to right in case he could see anything suspicious or abnormal. At the end of the hallway there were some doors; he didn't know what was waiting behind each door, doom or safety? He looked carefully at each door, which was the right door to safety...?

Emmanuel Lawal (11)

Tapton School, Sheffield

The Woods

The night had crept up on me! The tall spiky trees stood upwards like Guantanamo Bay prisoners on death row; I swivelled my body around, taking in my eerie surroundings. Soft muddy undergrowth beneath my feet; the rows of deathly trees stretched out towards the misty horizon! They were like a natural cage isolating me, and whatever else was out there, from the mostly sane world. I stood there quivering in jet-black wellies, pleading out in my mind to God, beckoning for Him to save me. A twig snapped behind me, I turned around. I wasn't alone anymore...

Eddie Slater (11)
Tapton School, Sheffield

The Chase

In the woods, I began to realise I was alone. It was getting dark when I heard something. I carried on. It came closer and I walked faster. I began to jog. It began to jog, slightly concerned I ran. It ran. Heart pounding I sprinted through the woods, twigs and branches gripped my hair and skin wrenching me backwards. In the distance, I heard an agonising cry. This meant it was getting closer. Gaining speed, it galloped through the eeriness of the late night air. I stumbled backwards, falling into its grasp. All I could think was *please*...

Rosie Allwood (12)
Tapton School, Sheffield

The Locket

She wasn't alone. She walked by the murky river despite being told not to many times by her parents. She didn't care. As she moved swiftly by the water, greeny eyes creepily rose to the surface. Her head jerked slightly as a twig crunched beneath her foot. She stepped onto the ancient, dilapidated bridge. It creaked. She reached for the locket that was hidden in her pocket. She blinked back tears as she opened it to reveal a handsome, young man. She closed her sapphire eyes. The locket slipped through her hands. Suddenly, she slid and fell to her death.

Samantha Doan (12)
Tapton School, Sheffield

The Kingdom Of Isolation

Home alone I heard a spine-chilling noise. *Knock! Knock!* Multiple emotions struck me. Maybe going on holiday was what I should've done. The face on the door handle followed my every move, all four walls in the room were closing in on me, like a kingdom of isolation. Movement of my feet were uncontrollable as they scampered to safety. Rasping noises penetrated my ears. The entire house was coming to life. I was no longer at peace. I was at torture. Slowly turning round my heart sank, knowing this was almost the end...

Alla Hamid (11)
Tapton School, Sheffield

The Stalking Night

I knocked on the door to the wooden haunted shed. No one answered. Despite being confident, I suddenly felt a cold chill run through my spine. I slowly crept round to the other side. To my right there was an old cracked window. I saw a glimpse of red pop up from the undergrowth below the window. I saw what looked like an Afro, big ears and then… That smile, I remember it from my nightmares. *Bang! Bang!* Before I could run I fell to the hard stone floor. I was never seen by anyone again.

Tom Fox (11)
Tapton School, Sheffield

Roller Raid

As the two friends stepped onto the spine-chilling roller coaster they took a quick glance at this colossal deathtrap. They felt deep scepticism but entered anyway. Eventually, the ride started and it cluttered from side to side. Many feet below them stood a wicked, vile man. At that very second Jane saw deep into his possessed soul and her heart jumped out of her chest. He took his murder weapon and made a life-threatening incision into the rusty metal. He was evil; he had been taken over by the Devil. *Creak!* Jane's heart sank as she fell to her death…

Lola Pinnock (11)
Tapton School, Sheffield

Escape

Moonlight bounces across the vast lake. Exploring every crevice of the tremendous cliffs of the east. To the west, trees stand like mountains. To the north, the safe haven, my only hope. There's no time to spare; I can already hear the distant, hallow screeches of those monsters. Plunging the paddle into the icy water once more; the boat surges forwards, descending into the mist. Its cold, dead fingers are quick to wrap around my body. What was protection, is now a labyrinth of gloom...
My heart stops. I'm too late. A bony hand encloses on my shoulder... They... have me...

Jack Binns
Tapton School, Sheffield

Tomorrow

I remember it like it was yesterday. Strolling along the pavement minding my own business, everything was going perfectly. At least for a while. I awkwardly slanted my head backwards to view my surroundings, when a dark figure caught the focus of my sight. I was way to elated to think anything negative. Oh why wasn't I more aware? Why couldn't I shake off the good mood and snap back to reality? It was then when silence dominated everything and a rough hand lay on my shoulder. Finally, the fear got to me. 'Young boy, tomorrow is a dark place.'

Bashdar Ali Abdullah
Tapton School, Sheffield

The Fallen Warrior

I stagger to the ground. My hands on my forehead, blood seeping through my fingers. I lay there, sand swirling in my face and surrounded by bones of fallen warriors. I will soon join them. The sand around me beginning to stain red and I know that no one is coming to help me. The shadows are too strong. We will be wiped out and remembered as the rebels; those who made a pointless attempt at freedom against their religion. Our story will not be told the same. Our story will be told by those who were not there.

Freddy Ortiz (14)
Tapton School, Sheffield

Dark!

Twit twoo, twit twoo, the owls go. Lonely owls go flying high around the rotten, worthless castle, as it comes alive. I walk on the uneven, treacherous grounds watching the castle's peepholes brighten. As bright as the moonlit sky; my eyes widen! The trees swaying side to side, *swish swoo,* it's magical. I hear crackling of dead crispy leaves. Is someone there? 'Hello?' I start walking rapidly, my heart pounding like a bass drum. 'Hello?' A shadow appears; a figure shadow. The castle still bright like the stars in the sky. Suddenly, the castle aggressively goes dark...

Holly Hunt (14)
Tapton School, Sheffield

The Ever-Watching Eyes

The white hot embers dwindled in the hearth, the grandfather clock chimed; but it didn't wake Skye. Whilst fast asleep, she was witnessing a terrible nightmare. She lay in bed, paralysed by terror. No sound could escape her mouth. Pairs of eyes began to glow in the dark; they were lava-red and tinged by psychotic rage. Their ruthless lust for blood was clear...

Skye woke with a start, her bed sheets were dripping with sweat. She scanned her room and was drawn to a fiery red glow. There they were, the eyes from her nightmare. Savage and unblinking.

Max William Altman (14)

Tapton School, Sheffield

Shadows

The day was slowly coming to an end, but the torrential rain wasn't. By this point I had lost Kylie in the ominous forest. As I promenaded further I heard rustling at both sides of me. *It must've been a dog*, I thought. The sound faded. All of a sudden I felt like I was surrounded by eerie creatures although nothing was insight. 'Something supernatural maybe? No, I have grown up here, it can't be.' The wind howling, the rustling blaring and rain deafening I turned; feeling it approach me.

Iqra Yousuf (14)

Tapton School, Sheffield

Anabeth And The Haunted Forest

As soon as I walked into the classroom, everyone started to laugh at me, I wondered why. As soon as I sat down people were talking about a scary forest in Wington Lane, which is where I live.

After school when I was walking home, I saw the terrifying forest everyone was talking about. I walked to the forest and it actually looked incredibly creepy. I heard a voice come from the other side of the forest. Suddenly, I bolted to see what it was. I then saw a note on the ground saying: 'You are in deep danger!'

Safa Farah (11)
Tapton School, Sheffield

Left Behind

As I finished up my after school detention, the lights flickered. Suddenly, it was pitch-black... Then I saw the caretaker under a flickering light. I called his name, he didn't respond. I started to get chills down my back. I turned, he said, 'Yes!'

'Nothing, sir.'

He shouted, 'Come here!' Despite that it was probably a harmless coincidence; my survival instincts kicked in. I ran for it. I heard footsteps creaking behind me. I bailed into the cafeteria. The lights flickered... There was no light. I felt a hand on my shoulder. 'Time to clean up kid.'

Sam Beaumont (11)
Tapton School, Sheffield

The Morning Walk

The glistening beams of sunlight wriggled through the branches, to light up the untouched, crisp forest floor. Matt was taking his girlfriend, Beth, on a early morning walk with their dog, Max. The walk had been delightful until Max ran off. They had been searching for hours, but hadn't got any closer to finding him. Then, suddenly, they heard a bark coming from behind them. The couple were relieved, they started running towards the sound of the barking, they had seen Max's tail wagging in the distance, they got closer and found him chewing on a human head.

Oliver Beaumont (14)

Tapton School, Sheffield

Hide-And-Seek

I ran through the eerie shadows that the ancient trees cast and tripped over the green, tangled bushes that were everywhere. Me and Kate were playing hide-and-seek in the woods. It was perfectly safe, wasn't it? Nothing bad had happened before. I jumped over the weak, rickety fence with a battered sign reading: *Keep Out!* I opened the unlocked door to the crumbling, tiny hut. I hid under a small, rotting desk and faced the mouldy walls. I heard the old door open. My heart pounded like a hammer. It wasn't Kate. 'Found you,' it whispered.

Maqaddas Ahmad (14)

Tapton School, Sheffield

Shadows

The dark shadows that had cast themselves between each eerie tree were enough for his fear to kick in. A momentary blinding light crept upon those living amongst the overgrown trees, trying to relieve Lewis from his gloomy depression; although it would last forever. The stench of the precarious figure's breath could be smelt as it lurched behind Lewis. Would his forever end soon? Shattered from the run he fell to his knees, whimpering, as he prepared himself for the figure to attack, when the realisation hit him; he was only running from the voices in his head.

Lucy Boyes (14)
Tapton School, Sheffield

It

Bodies lay mutilated on the floor, eyes crudely gouged from their socket, the twisted faces didn't portray pain, but fear. The lights flickered, sweat ran down my face. What was that? Singing? Down the hall came the soft singing of a nursery rhyme, 'Ring-a-ring o' roses'. Stepping through the ruptured forms, knee-deep on the floor, I spoke. 'Hello?' I was shaking now and then I saw it. *Chop, chop, chop*, down the knife went. I heard a scream and the singing stopped. It turned to look at me, smiled at me and lifted the rusty knife.

Archie Noble (14)
Tapton School, Sheffield

Night-Time Adventure

It was approaching midnight as the adventurous boys sneaked silently through the fields of swaying crops to the abandoned castle. Glittering moonlight stopped where the castle stood then portrayed a gloomy shadow hiding the sleeping town below. The creaky wooden door swung open; inviting the boys inside. *Bang!* The door slammed shut. The boys followed the damp, dingy corridors of the once proud castle. Every turn they made, got them more tangled in the never-ending web of pathways. Morning and the bright rays of sunlight peered over the hill. The boys however never peered back over the hill again...

Molly Twigg (15)
Tapton School, Sheffield

Death Note

It was a sunny day, a peaceful day, and a great day for Jimmy. It was his birthday. He had plans to go out with his family, after he had been out with his friends. He had arranged to meet there. When he got there he found his sister alone, crying with a note which said: 'If you want your parents alive you will have to kill your friends'. He then felt a bang on his head.
He woke up in relief but then found the note in his coat pocket, soaked in blood.

Joe Ollerenshaw (14)
Tapton School, Sheffield

The Secrets Of The Forest

The trees seemed to whisper to each other as if sharing a secret, but I wasn't in on that secret, at the time I didn't care. I'd never been this far in before, my footsteps marking untouched territory. I'd got used to the sounds of snapping twigs and squelching leaves. I took a step and basked in the sun rays, another one and I closed my eyes embracing it all. It was the next step that changed my life. It took me a while to realise the screaming was coming from me. I would never be the same again, never!

Jessica Silvester (14)
Tapton School, Sheffield

The Abandoned Mineshaft

It was a dark and rainy day, there were four men all in one car. One of the men was tall and worked as a businessman. He was the driver. He couldn't see the road properly, *bang!* The car crashed into a tree. They were all fine, they got out of the car to explore for shelter and came across an abandoned mineshaft. It had a thin piece of wood covering it with a sign on it which said: *Do Not Enter,* but the men didn't listen…

Salem Mahfoudh (14)
Tapton School, Sheffield

Snow

I trudged through the snow. My breath coming in short gasps, visible in the cold night air. I had been running for some time now, clutching the bite mark on my neck. I turned to see a shadow dart from one of the trees. That thing was here! I turned back round to run when something fell to the floor in front of me. I looked down in horror to see a mangled corpse lying in the snow. Before I could scream I was wrenched backwards and dragged through the snow. I clawed for a handhold, but to no avail…

Isabel Drakeford (14)

Tapton School, Sheffield

Crunch

Crunch, crunch, crunch, I run through the magnificent autumn colours on the golden floor. *Crunch, crunch, crunch,* I step precariously through the deep woodland. My feet poised on my tiptoes, I venture further into the wood. I see different colours, hear different sounds and smell different smells – maybe this is why it says: *No Entry. Crunch, crunch, crunch,* the piercing sound of broken branches beneath my feet as I trek to the wall. By then, I hear something… something special; something abnormal like me, something else is going *crunch, crunch, crunch!* Then, I feel something cold on my shoulder…

Matthew Lawrence (14)

Tapton School, Sheffield

Woken From Restless Sleep

He wouldn't stop. I tried, but he wouldn't listen. I helped him, yet I still wake up to screams. He always wanted money, sex or more of the things I don't want nor have. Today I woke to something different. I heard gags but didn't feel hands on my throat. I felt taps but not punches. As I stood over him, I proved that now he is feeble; powerless. I proved that he should've listened, should've accepted my help. But no, and as I watch over him, proving I am now superior, I watch the drug overdose take his life.

Lucas Parker (14)
Tapton School, Sheffield

The Witches' Hour

The dilapidated castle covered the small town of Longdale with an eerie shadow. I felt a chill go down my spine. The story of the witch never scared me, till now. I was getting closer to the castle, with my torch I could see the shattered windows and the colossal door. I was frightened. The archaic clock chimed 12. The witches' hour. I could hear the distant howls of the grotesque beasts. Those distant howls were no longer in the distance, they were getting closer by the second. Then they were surrounding me. My torch suddenly went off.

Thomas Steven Frow (14)
Tapton School, Sheffield

A World Away

It's her, from Todd's party. She's vibrant; shinning more than my memory can recall. A sea of gold flowing down her back with waves of mesmerising colour. She reaches out with her delicate hands while a different pair of hands stab me with a knife. Two memories at once. It's as if time is breaking down. The girl leans closer, and I feel the warmth radiating from her body. Then doctors, nurses and Mother crying. Two worlds at once. Her pristine face demands my attention. My heart stops as gentle lips kiss me. 'Gone,' the doctor sighs. 'I'm sorry, madam.'

Tom Shaw (15)

Tapton School, Sheffield

Matt?

It was a dark dismal day, sleet tumbling from the heavens. Matt wasn't far behind; but I wasn't going to wait for him in the rain. I had told him I would wait for him in the dilapidated community hall. The solid wood doors were hefty to move. Inside the bleak hall there was nothing, it used to be place of activity and joy and now is forgotten. As I explored I heard the weighty door creak open, I turned and I saw dangling in the wind from the mouldy lifeless roof was... 'Matt?'

Oliver Rogerson (14)

Tapton School, Sheffield

Out Of Nowhere

As the kid entered the haunted house, the pair of eyes watched him. The eyes didn't leave him until he entered the haunted house. The house was so silent you could hear nothing. The kid looked behind, he knew there was something but wasn't sure what it was...
'Twas a very loud noise. You could hear its loud deep footsteps. The boy didn't know what to do. He picked up the phone. Suddenly, a little rock out of nowhere had hit the phone. The phone dropped with a thundering sound from outside.

Isra Abdalhafiz (12)
Tapton School, Sheffield

A Spooky Alley

I impatiently pace up and down waiting for my friend. I enter the dark and gloomy passage. I'm terrified. Suddenly, light streams into the alley I can see but I wish I couldn't as moonlight makes terrifying shadows. The moon's big, round, cold face watching me. Watching how I react. I hold in my blood-curdling screams. *Clatter, bang, miaow.* A cat nudges the metal bin lid. The moonlight reflects off the lid like a disco ball. Then, from nowhere, a ghostly, eerily, white figure hovers across the cold, hard floor; it sends a shiver up my spine. What is it?

Sophie Ellin (14)
Tapton School, Sheffield

Castle

The moonlight illuminated the sky above the dry ruins of the castle, casting an eerie shadow to one side that hid all the secrets of the century. She walked up to it slowly; hands trembling as they come in contact with the rusty doorknob. The ancient door gave a creak as she pushed her way in. The only light was from the moon, twisting its way through the cracks. There was a spectacular, old mirror in the corner. She crept up to it, intrigued by its natural beauty. Suddenly, a shadow appeared behind her shoulder. Then she was gone...

Hannah Campbell (14)
Tapton School, Sheffield

Your Own Worst Enemy Is Yourself

Here was a man that would pound the streets and criticise everything a man or woman would wear, like he was the next Gok Wan. No one liked this man and one day the town had had enough. People were shouting, 'Kill the man, throw him out of town!' So they did. He moved to a near place. The man was called Steve.
As soon as he stepped out of his car, one man shouted, 'You look like a clown with those shoes.' This man was also called Steve. Steve always wondered if he had a doppelgänger. He knows now.

Alex Whelan (15)
Tapton School, Sheffield

Bliss In Concealed Desolations

We don't talk about others; we just dance with our own demons,
hearts intoxicated with the deepest desires to drown you with us.
Don't be scared. It's only blood. Dark, gooey, wet, dripping blood;
engulfing us in its metallic, fruity aroma. We can't explain. You won't
understand. Run; cowardice will coil your mind in circles until you
break. Hide; the shadows will delude you as they serve us. Eventually,
fear will consume you until surrender.
'So dark. So deep. The secrets that we keep...' We don't talk about
others; that's for the weak.

Lisandra Chikwa (15)
Tapton School, Sheffield

The Puzzle

Jigsaw pieces, strewn about in front of my trembling hands. No matter
how hard I tried, they would not fit together. Screaming in frustration,
the more I tried, the smaller the pieces they became. I had seen the
jigsaw pieces assembled once, her golden hair shining radiantly in
the sun. Now there was blood in that wheat-coloured hair, and the
jigsaw pieces wouldn't fit together. Some of the jigsaw pieces were
covered in that blood. Perhaps that's why the pieces would still not fit
together?

Isobel Robson (14)
The McAuley Catholic High School, Doncaster

I've Got You

Dark. It was pitch-black. The air was thin, cold and bitter. I tried to catch my breath and stand up but couldn't. Where was I? My wrists and ankles tied up by heavy chains. Hopelessly yanking on my arms and legs, trying to break free until I bled sore. Suddenly, I heard an awful voice that seemed to be getting closer. I couldn't work out where I was. The voice was creepy and kept repeating, 'I'm going to get you.' I loudly called for help. A cold, spine-chilling hand grabbed me. 'I've got you!' a cold voice claimed.

Luciana Randall (14)
The McAuley Catholic High School, Doncaster

Spine-Chillers

Slowly, the large oak door creaks open with a spine-chilling noise! The stairs are sitting there staring at me. It may be my imagination but I can hear the stairs whispering scarily, 'Don't go up, she'll ruin you.' I take a step in the house and the entire floor shakes beneath my feet. As all my weight jolts down my left leg, I feel a tingle creep up my spine. The whole staircase squeaks at me like dying, eerie mice. Then, a deep black shadow appears from nowhere in front of my petrified eyes. Then, *bam*, it all goes black...

Luke Whitworth (11)
The McAuley Catholic High School, Doncaster

Spine-Chillers

In the space-like prison of darkness, the malicious reapers cried as the silver-coated wolves began howling in the light of the glimmering moon.The creaky oak door swung wide open as ghosts rapidly leaked out of the doorway, filled with complete evil. Suddenly, I heard footsteps walking across the wooden floor, steadily, as if they knew something was here. There was a slight grunt and heavy breathing. The mysterious sounds came from a dog-like creature which I saw rapidly run from one side of the room to the other. I wasn't sure how to escape...

Amaad Hassan (12)
The McAuley Catholic High School, Doncaster

Spine-Chillers

It was a dark, ominous winter night. I was walking home from school when I noticed something following me; it was not the average size for a human, instead it was much taller. As soon as it was about to touch me I looked over my shoulder; it disappeared. That was the point I knew something was out of the ordinary. Something had to be done! I started to run, but it kept on following me at the same speed. Suddenly, a hand reached out and grabbed me – I realised it was the thing behind me. It was my backpack.

Luke William Black (11)
The McAuley Catholic High School, Doncaster

Spine-Chillers

Meredith crept along the creaky wooden floor, tiptoeing, trying not to wake the spirits of the past. The room was filled with the smell of dusty sheets, a bit like the ones covering the rooms belonging to the mystical monsters. Opening her eyes, she discovered a photo frame with a picture of a ghost in it! 'Hello Meredith, I see you have come to stay and become a ghost with us, let me kill you and we can live happily together,' spoke the picture.
'No!' said Meredith. Out of the black door she ran. 'You'll never capture me, I'm invincible!'

Lucy Olivia Boyack (11)
The McAuley Catholic High School, Doncaster

Spine-Chillers

Eeek goes the floorboards of the new house. 'The Googlies' carved on the rock in the garden. It's one of those houses you normally find next to a graveyard... 'Hmm, I wonder what's in the attic?' I ask myself repeatedly. Since we first moved in a week ago I already feel at home but the attic is the only place I haven't explored. The question haunts me so I decide to disobey my mum's words and see what my mum's been hiding from me. The door creaks open. I reach the top and something strange lurks... Argh!

Logan Cronin (11)
The McAuley Catholic High School, Doncaster

Spine-Chillers!

It was a dark, foggy night, a full moon. The light shone through the fog, making the surroundings eerily bright. Only the flapping of an owl's wing flew through the air. Dark grass rustled as a young girl slumped to the mysterious silhouette in the distance. A faint growl lingered behind her. Soft, comforting fur brushed against her arm, or did it? The next thing she knew, she was looking at the brown mud below. A sharp pain sped through her body and just as soon as it had come, it had gone. 'Help! Help me, please!' Blackness everywhere.

Elizabeth Matthews (11)
The McAuley Catholic High School, Doncaster

Spine-Chillers

The new house was amazing! It may have been old, but so beautiful. My bedroom was my favourite part of the house, Dad had decorated it just as I wanted. Everyone loved it, there was just one thing that kept bothering me, every time I walked past the basement door, the wooden door was locked, no one knew where the key was. We were told by the estate agent not to open it. When we asked why, the only answer we got was a cold glare. I guess I'll never know why there were noises from the basement every night.

Livia Haider (12)
The McAuley Catholic High School, Doncaster

Spine-Chillers

She crept along the oak-wood floor, nervously glancing side to side. It was pitch-black. She tiptoed through a door. The building was colossal. Brodie hated horror stories with a passion and now, it was like she was in one herself. She blinked and when the petrified girl opened her eyes, she found about a hundred tiny pairs of eyes staring at her disturbingly. She screamed, and ran as fast as her feet and legs would take her. Suddenly, *bang,* she fell and tried picking herself up, it was too late...

Karolina Szykula (11)
The McAuley Catholic High School, Doncaster

Spine-Chillers

So I walked along when something stabbed at my poor swollen ankle... a claw of some sort. I only saw something red glisten in the corner of my eye. It looked like... fingernails. Curved and curled. I hurried on, trying not to think about it. That night as I went to sleep, I heard something. It came from the corner of the room. I sat up straight away and flicked on the light. Something was sat there. I shivered and then I walked over shaking...

Brodilyee Aimson (11)
The McAuley Catholic High School, Doncaster

Spine-Chillers

I glare at a bright light, haunting me to the death. *Tick-tock, tick-tock.* My head's going round and round, everything is weird! *Bang, crash! What is that?* I think, as I wander through the streets of NYC. My head in the clouds...

By the way, my name's Faith and this is my wonderful world of weirdness! This always happens to me, my friend, who is actually a doll helps me through the times. Can you actually believe it? He moves and he wants to kill me! I get used to to it though because I am actually dead!

Freya Bouse (12)
The McAuley Catholic High School, Doncaster

Spine-Chillers

Appearing from the darkness, the vile creature made a piercing scream like a malevolent teacher. Freezing goosebumps were quickly spotted screeching on my body, trying to escape for their lives. I was exceptionally petrified, I couldn't move my body, not an inch. I was prepared to faint; hope was not present in my fragile form. The vicious monster approached me, it was ready to pounce; there was nowhere to hide. Laughing nastily, the out of this world brute seemed almost immortal. 'Please don't hurt me!' I cried. I had already given up before a mysterious figure came and saved me.

Alexander Sadeghi (11)
The McAuley Catholic High School, Doncaster

Spine-Chillers...

As I walk down the hall, everything is silent... *Boom! Crash! Bang!* The school begins to shake. I run as fast as my legs can take me and smash through the doors to exit my school. As I turn, I see LA being burnt down, I cannot believe what has happened and I cannot believe who would do this. My legs automatically rush home to try to find my mother (Emily) and baby sister (Freya). Their bodies lay silent, and still. A man walks up to me and shoots me. I lay still, wondering what has become of the world...

Faith Glossop (11)
The McAuley Catholic High School, Doncaster

It's Time

I turned and looked at the clock... It was 2.30, I snuggled down again wondering what had woken me... When I heard a noise. It was a dripping sound. I thought that I had left the water running. My tears were burning me. The Devil was helping me. Hell was waiting for me. The Lord of Evil stepped down from Hell to welcome me. The Lord of Hell knew me! My dark mind was controlling all the dark now! Too scary! Too real!

Manal Awadh (12)
Yewlands Academy, Sheffield

Francescal's Final Memory

There was a girl called Francescal, it's a strange name for a child! She heard a noise outside in the wilderness and her curiosity got the best of her. She strolled along the stony pathway as the sinister trees scraped against the wind. Francescal felt a punishing hand on her shoulder. She turned to a spine-chilling man behind her. His face was mislaid, his clothes were ragged and dark. A shiver went down her spine as blood dripped from her eyes into his cold, polluted hand. Her final memory was of her stolen eyes looking down at her corpse.

Holly Fraser (12)
Yewlands Academy, Sheffield

Knock At The Door

One day there was a knock at the door so I went and answered it and that is when it all happened. There I was tied up in the back of someone's van with my mother and father. I heard a police siren but I didn't know whether to scream because they might stop the van. Then me and my family would get murdered, but I still did and the police heard me. The driver in the van zoomed down the road and crashed into a wall. I never saw my mother and father again from that day.

Lily Lambert (12)
Yewlands Academy, Sheffield

The Five Night Stop

One stormy night, at a local pizzeria, there was five animatronics: Freddy, Bonnie, Chica and Foxy but there was a secret one that nobody knew about, until this very day! He was called Golden Freddy, he was just a plain endoskeleton. There had been rumours about a current murderer who killed five children. Everyone was screaming but the golden suit was asked to lure the children into the 'Safety Room'. At that very time a guy called Michael Schmidt was there and suddenly the power went out and Freddy came and screamed ferociously. 'Argh!'

Courtney Sylvia Ann Pickstone (12)
Yewlands Academy, Sheffield

A Girl And Her Dog

There was a little girl called Daisy, she was eight years old and she had a dog called Ralph. It was night-time and Daisy was laid in bed with her dog laid on the floor. Daisy was fast asleep when a burglar came and took her dog and hung him from the roof. Daisy put her hand down and the burglar licked it.
Two hours later, Daisy woke up to a loud noise. She heard a *drip-drop, drip-drop*. The noise was blood dripping from the dangling dead dog.

Jessica Hill (12)
Yewlands Academy, Sheffield

Est.1991

YOUNG WRITERS
INFORMATION

We hope you have enjoyed reading this book – and
that you will continue to in the coming years.

If you're a young writer who enjoys reading and creative writing, or
the parent of an enthusiastic poet or story writer, do visit our website
www.youngwriters.co.uk. Here you will find free
competitions, workshops and games, as well as
recommended reads, a poetry glossary and our blog.

If you would like to order further copies of this
book, or any of our other titles, then please give us
a call or visit **www.youngwriters.co.uk.**

Young Writers
Remus House
Coltsfoot Drive
Peterborough
PE2 9BF
(01733) 890066 / 898110
info@youngwriters.co.uk